UNCA DAVE'S WILDERNESS

ESSENTIAL PROSE SERIES 208

Canada Council for the Arts
Conseil des Arts du Canada

ONTARIO ARTS COUNCIL
CONSEIL DES ARTS DE L'ONTARIO
an Ontario government agency
un organisme du gouvernement de l'Ont

Canada

Guernica Editions Inc. acknowledges the support of the Canada Council for the Arts and the Ontario Arts Council. The Ontario Arts Council is an agency of the Government of Ontario.

We acknowledge the financial support of the Government of Canada.

UNCA DAVE'S WILDERNESS

david sapin

GUERNICA EDITIONS

TORONTO—CHICAGO—BUFFALO—LANCASTER (U.K.)

2023

Guernica Founder: Antonio D'Alfonso

Michael Mirolla, editor
Interior and cover design: Errol F. Richardson
Guernica Editions Inc.
287 Templemead Drive, Hamilton, ON L8W 2W4
2250 Military Road, Tonawanda, N.Y. 14150-6000 U.S.A.
www.guernicaeditions.com

Distributors:
Independent Publishers Group (IPG)
600 North Pulaski Road, Chicago IL 60624
University of Toronto Press Distribution (UTP)
5201 Dufferin Street, Toronto (ON), Canada M3H 5T8

First edition.
Printed in Canada.

Legal Deposit—Third Quarter
Library of Congress Catalog Card Number: 9781771838085
Library and Archives Canada Cataloguing in Publication
Title: Unca Dave's wilderness / David Sapin.
Names: Sapin, David, author.
Series: Essential prose series ; 208.
Description: Series statement: Essential prose series ; 208 | Short stories.
Identifiers: Canadiana (print) 20230176194 | Canadiana (ebook) 20230180884 | ISBN 9781771838085 (softcover) | ISBN 9781771838092 (EPUB)
Classification: LCC PS8637.A695 U53 2023 | DDC C813/.6—dc23

For my nephew Matti who was always thrilled
by my stupid complicated inventions
that served absolutely no useful purpose whatsoever
but always made him laugh.

And for Amanda who is batshit crazy
but smarter than all of us put together.

TABLE OF CONTENTS

MICE

I LIKE MICE.

As long as they are outside, in which case they are wildlife.

Inside the house, though, they are vermin. In fact, anything that typically lives outside is wildlife and becomes vermin as soon as it transitions from outside the walls of my house to the side that I prefer to live in. Unless I have specifically invited them to do so and they agree to abide by certain house rules. But I still like them.

One day the wife declares that we have got mice. As proof, she holds up the bread basket that sits permanently on the kitchen counter to reveal two or three mouse turds. The evidence is incontrovertible; immediate action must be taken.

First on the agenda: mention it casually to someone that you know.

"Oh, yeah. Been there. The first thing that you have to do is buy a shitload of rat poison and spread it absolutely all over the place!"

OK. Any other bright ideas?

Since it was urgent, I went to the hardware store and bought a spring-loaded trap. It was against my better judgement, since I already knew precisely what the outcome would be. But it was imperative that I show the wife that I was proactive, lest she lose faith in my ability to protect her from this real and imminent threat.

Sure enough, the next morning, there was the mouse, his tiny skull smashed by the cold steel bar, his little exorbitant red eyes each with a tiny cartoon X drawn over them, a few drops of rusty brown mouse blood trickling from his fuzzy ears and white-whiskered nose. My only thought was about the microsecond between the moment that the mouse realized that he had made an error in judgement and the moment when his consciousness was permanently obliterated.

I tossed the entire murderous mess onto the breakfast table and said, "There you go. No more mouse. Happy?"

Obviously not, by the look on her face, and not because there was a crushed mouse sitting next to her wheat germ and brown toast. It was guilt from having ordered the execution.

"Are there any more?" she inquired timidly.

I couldn't say. Maybe there was only one. But typically, when there's one, there's a shitload.

"I dunno," I lied, shrugging. "Let's wait till tomorrow."

Sure enough, the next morning there was fresh mouse poo on the kitchen counter and under the sink.

"Are you gonna catch them?" the wife whimpered.

"Sure," I said, bluffing. "Piece of cake."

"You won't use the trap? Please?"

Aha. Exactly what I needed to hear. I wouldn't hurt a hair on any of their heads, but I had to sacrifice at least one to the guillotine to get my wife to plead with me to catch them humanely. Now it was a fair fight, mano a mano, hominidis contra la musca, and let the last mammalian vertebrate standing lord it over his conquered adversary! Let the games begin!

Of course, I could have gone back to the hardware store and bought a humanitarian trap for twenty bucks, but they are so mundane and utilitarian and ugly, and where is the challenge in that?

So, I decided to design and build my own trap.

The first four prototypes failed miserably, and a month later the mouses were still romping about the house as if they owned it, which, as far as they were concerned, they did.

But then I nailed it. Or almost.

I built a tiny box out of scrap wood, barely a few inches per side, with a postage-stamp sized guillotine door that was held up by a thread that went through a tiny hole in the wall of the tiny room and held a piece of bait on the inside. When the mouse entered the box and ate the bait, the thread was released and the door slid down to cover the aperture, thus trapping the mouse. Voila!

In theory. In reality, what happened is that the trapped mouse quickly figured out that the string controlled the door, and that by pulling on the loose end he could open and close the door at will. Not only did he do that, but he also managed to wedge the thread into a tiny crack in the wood, and thus lock the door permanently open so that he could scamper in and out of the trap with impunity.

The damned thing is the size of my pinky, and it managed to outthink a man who had studied engineering at McGill. I smiled to myself. If I catch that little bugger, I will teach it to play chess, and it will probably beat me.

I shortened the thread so that when the mouse took the bait the end would be pulled outside of the box, but the mouse figured out how to push the door up from the inside. So, then I had to invent a locking device that would slide down onto the closed door. I used a large paper clip, a pop rivet and some small washers, and it actually worked.

The next morning, after almost two months of trying, I actually caught my first live mouse!

I proudly displayed my prey on the breakfast table. You could actually see the vanquished animal cowering in the darkest recesses of the box, because I had equipped the roof with a removable transparent piece of plastic.

"Wonderful," the wife quipped. "Now what the hell are you gonna do with it?"

Wow. Good point. I had been so preoccupied with catching the little bugger that I hadn't thought the thing all the way through. Obviously, I couldn't leave it in the box. And I couldn't just toss it out the door; it was stone cold dead winter out there. Three feet of hard frozen snow and thirty below in the shade. Turfing it out would be worse than smashing its head in with the spring trap. I had to keep it in the house until spring.

Louise (a.k.a. the wife) gave me a plastic storage bin that is supposed to contain documents. It's pretty big, bigger than your microwave oven, and it has plastic flaps on the top that interlock, so it seemed unlikely that the mouse could actually escape.

I parked the bin in the basement, threw in a small handful of sunflower seeds and a tiny bowl of water, dumped the mouse inside and closed up the top. I then reset the trap under the sink in case there were any more mice, which I suspected there were.

The next morning, two things happened. First of all, there was another mouse in my trap under the sink. I mentally beat my breast and howled like Tarzan. Victory! The second thing is, when I brought my captive down to the basement to join his kin in the big plastic box, the box was, well, empty. No mouse. The little bugger had absconded from the premises.

I looked at the box, then at the trap. The trapped mouse was anxiously looking at me through the transparent plexiglass roof.

It dawned on me then that I had probably just trapped the same mouse, and if I just parked it back into the same cage, it would perform exactly the same miracle as the day before and simply pull another Houdini on me.

I dumped the mouse back into the plastic box, put a plank and a few bricks on top, and then duct-taped the entire outside rim of the box, hoping only that the poor little bastard wouldn't run out of air. The cage was hermetically sealed. Then I drove to work.

When I got home later that day, I went to inspect the cage. There was no mouse in it.

I was piqued, but I had to re-strategize. If I wanted a successful outcome for me, I had to start thinking like a mouse. Two days running, I caught the mouse, put it in the cage, and then lost the mouse.

So, the trap, as far as the mouse was concerned, was no longer a threat, but merely a gateway to a big box full of food and water that it could, apparently, easily escape from. Given that data, the mouse was probably eager to be trapped. The trap was merely a toy, and this was all just an enjoyable experience.

Ironically, I actually felt the same. But there had to be an outcome, and the only one that I could envisage was me winning. (I'm sure the mouse had his own ideas.)

So, Friday night I set the trap again, knowing that Saturday morning I could watch the little guy and figure out how he had escaped the big box.

Sure enough, the next morning the same caramel-coloured little piece of fur was in the trap under the sink, and I dutifully transferred him to his basement prison. But this time I pulled up a stool and watched, and this was my home movie for the next hour and a half.

The mouse's Thunderdome cage was huge. Imagine yourself inside a plastic box the size of a city block, twelve stories high, and the walls are smooth and vertical, and the roof is sealed. How can you escape? You can't, obviously, and you will surely die there.

Unless you are a mouse.

The first ten or fifteen minutes of my movie saw the mouse running around the floor of his cage, occasionally standing up and sniffing the wall with his wiggly nose and stiff white whiskers.

Last act of a desperate mouse? No. Painstaking calculations in preparation for the Great Mouse Escape.

The first few jumps were just to evaluate how much spring was required to get to the top. The next dozen or so were just to figure out the angle of the tiny claws in order to hook onto the upper lip of the box, just under the lid, and how much space there was between the rim and the lid, so that the mouse didn't bang its tiny head on the way up. That took fifty tries, maybe more.

The next step was to hook up the two tiny front paws to the top of the box. That done, the mouse then let go of the left hand and hung there from the other tiny paw. Then it began to swing its body, left to right, more and more energetically, like a tiny pendulum, until its back foot slid up and connected with the upper lip of the box and took hold.

I was hypnotized by these miniature heroic gymnastics. You try jumping up the face of a twelve-story building fifty times on the off-chance that you might attain the roof by your fingernails.

So now the mouse is hanging horizontally to the upper rim of the box, using only its two right limbs, and slowly trundling forward, sniffing the duct-taped joint every millimeter of the way. Occasionally it fails and falls back to the floor, but it immediately starts over the entire process, having learned and memorized what to do, and what not to do.

Eventually the mouse comes to a corner, where the space between the rim and the top is marginally wider. We are talking millimeters here. Its hands are carbon copies of your own, but tinier than a match head, and maybe with a bit more fur.

After five hundred attempts and 499 failures, the mouse has identified a microscopic failure in my defense system and exploited it. It chews a tiny hole in the duct tape and squeezes through, as if it were made of toothpaste.

The mouse has escaped, once again. Chess would not be a challenge for that little thing. Blindfold multiple speed chess while simultaneously running the Ironman marathon, maybe, but nothing less.

Shit. Now I have to not only trap the little thing permanently, but I also have to build a suitable house to keep it in AND keep it intellectually and physically stimulated until the snow melts. Am I up to the challenge?

POO YAH! Come on down, you rodent from hell, and I'll show you how we deal with cute furry caramel-coloured vermin!

So, I built a mouse terrarium from scrap and I eventually parked three mice in it, and fortunately they were all boys otherwise I would have had a population crisis. And I filled that space with toys and food and even got grass growing in there and I incorporated an air conditioner made from leftover computer fans and other components.

Eventually, spring sprang and the tiny guests had to get sprung. So, on a warm May morning I parked the whole shitload on the edge of the deck and opened the door.

By sundown the mice were still in their man-made house, reluctant to leave. Can you blame them? Free room and board, and absolutely no predators. Well, almost none. My cat Max the Manx used to watch them all the time; the mouse-terrarium was his favourite TV show. But by then Max had retired from his illustrious career as a relentless predator, and he was just mildly amused by little furry things scurrying randomly about on the other side of the plexiglass screen.

So, by sundown the mice were still parked inside their luxury mouse condo, so I trundled the whole shitload down to the barn and parked it on the floor.

And sure enough, by the next morning, the little buggers had flown the coop. And I can tell you exactly why.

Estrogen. Smell of female.

After being cooped up for three months, the poor bastards just wanted to get laid. I think I probably would have done exactly the same.

SHOES

I LIKE SHOES.

For lots of people, they are a fashion accessory. To me, they are just tools. They protect my feet from the hostilities of the outside world.

But what happens when you only own one pair, or none at all?

Sainte-Catherine Street West, Montreal. Downtown.

The old man squatted on the sidewalk, his back against the wall. A cardboard coffee cup sat between his knees, a few coins at the bottom anchoring it from the icy November wind. Nobody noticed him, not even me.

A cold mist was falling. It would soon congeal to freezing rain. Back then I was eating out of dumpsters myself, and squatting in an unheated shed in an alleyway with no electricity or water.

I hadn't eaten since that morning, and dark was falling.

Shit, I thought, and turned around. I sat next to the old man, mimicking his barely comfortable status, and stared off across the street in silent complicity.

People walked by, normal, well-fed people with nice dry winter boots and warm coats and manicured nails and fresh hairdos. I could smell the women's perfume as they wafted by. We were a month from Christmas, and the street wore a festive attitude.

Cars drove past. Men cruised along in luxury sedans, their comfortable encapsulated environments safely sealed off from our own alternate reality. Wearing sixty-dollar power ties and expensive watches and nifty after-shave and Serengeti sunglasses, even though it was dark outside.

We were invisible to all of them, and that suited me fine.

I pulled a scrunched-up cigarette from my pocket, my last one, and struck a match, still dry enough to spark.

I took a few drags, then silently handed it to the old man. As I did so I noticed a cherry-coloured cancerous growth hanging from his right cheek, about the size of a plum. I also noticed that he smelled like piss and shit and vomit and gangrene and mold and death. The last thing that I noticed was that he was wearing plastic beach thongs on his feet.

The old man handed me back the cigarette and I enjoyed a few last puffs.

Then I finally broke the silence.

"You got no shoes", I said.

He shrugged.

The cold drizzle hugged us like a disease.

I looked at my own feet. Brown patent leather loafers with worn leather soles, but still intact. Expensive when new, but already third-hand when I got them, and I had personally almost loved them to death. I loved those mules, mostly because they were the only ones that I owned, and despite the stains and scratches they were still very decently wearable.

I put my foot up against his. It looked like a reasonable match.

Shit! I thought. What would fucking li'll' baby Jesus do?

So, I took off my beloved shoes and peeled off my stinky old socks, then handed them to the old man.

"Here," I said.

For the first time he actually turned and looked at me. He hesitated, and I had to shove the footwear at him before he reluctantly accepted the gift.

He discarded his beachwear, pulled on my stinky old socks, and then slipped his gnarly old feet into the shoes.

"Good?" I asked.

He nodded and smiled. Poor old bastard. He'll be dead before spring. They'll find his frozen corpse in an alleyway with my shoes on his feet, and no one will ever know, or care.

I had five kliks to walk back to my own *piaule*, and the sidewalk was beginning to freeze. But I didn't feel the cold hard cement on my naked toes.

I was walking on air.

MICKEY MOUSE

I LIKE MICKEY MOUSE.

During my two years as an itinerant in Montreal, I had the privilege to interact with a number of wonderful people. We formed a community, completely cut off from mainstream society and yet entirely dependent on it. The flagrant waste that we blamed them for was precisely the resource that kept us alive.

Here is an outline of the characters that made up our community. I never ever learned anyone's last name:

Christian

Chris was a *calèche* driver in Quebec City. He earned a good wage, enjoyed a lavish lifestyle, lived with a good woman.

One day he just dropped everything and hitchhiked to Montreal. He squatted in a boarded-up house in Chinatown, where he lived for almost twenty years. The man was a genius with an IQ far above the norm.

We routinely collaborated on performance art projects at the Montreal punk/underground/alternative venue *Les Foufounes Électriques*, gathering random bits of trash from the back alleys on our way to the events, lest we lack raw materials to create our art.

Walter

Walter came from Winnipeg. He had inherited a huge swath of totally worthless bug-infested swampland in the wilderness somewhere up north of Saskatchewan. It took three days to get there; there were no roads. Walter dreamed of the day when he could move there permanently and live off the land, and I hope his wish came true, although I doubt it.

Walter was a professional urban scavenger. He could find anything. Milk, eggs, toys, shoes, winter coats. Salami. A piano. A screwdriver. Socks. Eyeglasses. A box of nails. Diapers. Eyeliner. A needle and thread. A dictionary. Anything.

The Carolines

There were two.

One dark-haired beauty of about 22; the other a tall scrawny blonde with the sad eyes. Both were unwed mothers with beautiful pre-school boys, and both were squatting in abandoned buildings on the margins of Chinatown.

The dark-eyed beauty went on to a spectacular career as a professional glass-blower. We were not only witnesses, but participants in her apprenticeship. When we learned that she was a candidate for one of a very limited number of places in a new school set up in an old fire hall in Old Montreal, we all scrambled to cobble together a reasonably convincing portfolio of references and diplomas that clinched her position.

The scrawny blonde with the sad eyes once saved me from a broken leg.

Benoit

Benoit was a young itinerant who was totally devoted to the two women and their kids, even though he was neither father nor lover. Using only garbage, he built a fenced-in playground on a vacant lot with slides and swings and toys. The site became an underground fully supervised educational day care center for other underprivileged single mothers in the neighbourhood. Walter supplied the necessary educational material; books and toys, as well as clothing and shoes. Where he got them, we never asked. We just asked, and he showed up with them.

Magalie

What can I say? Magalie was an elf, a fairy. A tiny little woman with a shy smile and bright eyes, bursting with talent and enthusiasm but seriously burdened by self-doubt and anxiety. Part of the reason may have been that she had a vagina about the diameter of an HB pencil, which put a serious limit on her options for intimacy.

Every year, just before Christmas, she got us all, the street people, high-paying day jobs playing Disney Characters for corporate family Christmas parties. All of the young women got to dress up as Disney fairies and princesses, and they looked so seductive that you just wanted to lure them back into the locker room, but we all had jobs to do.

The clients provided the costumes, and Walter would always come through with appropriate makeup, jewellery, shoes and accessories. And I typically played Mickey Mouse, which is not as much fun as it sounds. With the giant Styrofoam head and the coat tails, it gets boiling hot in there, especially when every single three-year-old in the room wants you to take them in your arms and hug them and swing them around and let them pee on you. They actually believe that you are the real bona fide Mickey, so you have to talk to them in a squeaky voice and try to sound like Mickey Mouse through the sweltering Styrofoam head.

At least they didn't ask for autographs.

It was hard work, but we were paid cash money and we all rose to the occasion. But above all, we were valorized. We were treated with humanity, and invited to the party, and respected as guests, and validated as contributors to the festivities.

I thank the persons that organized those events, even though I have no idea who they were. A thousand other catering opportunities were available to them, but they chose to hire street people, dress them up as princesses and elves and childhood icons, allow them to have intimate contact with real people and their children, then feed them like royalty and give them all luxurious doggie bags full of left-over roast chicken and cake and cookies and candy, and stuff their pockets with bills a week before Christmas and then send them off with a heartfelt "Thank you."

I'm sure those people, after the event, looked at each other and said, "I wish we could have done more."

And so did we. Not expect more, but, to contribute more.

CATS

I LIKE CATS.

I've owned shitloads of them. They are all dead now, except for one. His name is Ti-Lou, which doesn't mean anything at all except maybe mini-wolf or something like that.

Like every other cat that I have known, he is an abject hypocrite. If he wants kibble or a valet to open the door, then he is all over me, purring like there's no tomorrow. But if I want to pet him while he snores away on my favourite chair, he will gladly claw my eyes out and then go back to sleep.

Yesterday I buried another one of my cats in the garden. His name was Ti-Nou, which doesn't mean anything at all, unless you understand the context. So, let's go.

Back in 2008, we still rented movies on DVD from the store, and when we were done watching them, we brought them back, usually the next day.

The next day was Sunday in mid-August. The video store was a twenty-minute drive from my home, and I drove it in a Honda civic hatchback that was already twenty years old. Manual choke, and no AC, so to keep cool in summer you hand-cranked the windows to let in the breeze, and when you parked it, you left it like that to prevent the internal temperature from rising high enough to bake a cake.

On the way home, I heard some unusual, high-pitched

squeaking noises that I naturally attributed to some kind of mechanical failure, like used brakes or a leaky fan belt.

But after I got home and parked the car and killed the engine, the squeaky noises continued. Since the car was filled with garbage, it took a few minutes of rummaging before I put my hands on a tiny, black-and-white fur ball that someone had casually tossed through the rolled-down window of my car while I was in the video store.

What you got there? My wife asked.

I dunno, I replied, holding up the tiny, squeaky thing by the scruff. Looks like a baby cat.

What are we supposed to do with it? she inquired.

I dunno. I guess I can just bash its head in with a hammer, or tie it up in a bag and throw it under the wheels of the school bus tomorrow morning. Or we can keep it. You decide.

It's a fucking newborn baby kitten. What would you have done?

So, the next morning Louise swaddles it up in a blankie and hauls it down to the vet.

The prognosis is ugly. The tiny ball of fur and razor claws is actually ataxic, which means that at birth his spinal cord was stretched and broken, and that he is permanently paralyzed at the hips and probably has other serious neurological problems.

The vet was clear and frank. If you don't put him down immediately, then at least do not get too attached to this animal. He will die shortly, and it won't be pretty.

OK, doc. Give him his vaccination shots, and give me the bill. That toxic furball is coming home with me.

For the first four months, that animal hid in places that we never knew, and crept out at night to feed and drink, when the entire house was quiet.

Eventually Louise caught him, and she massaged his back and stretched his legs until he could actually stand up on his own, although he never ever learned to walk straight. He would typically stumble about like a drunkard, crashing into the walls and sliding around on the floor like an amateur skater.

He would try to scratch his ears with his back paw, but it would just spin around in the air like some demonic pendulum from hell. Then he would look at us with an expression that said, "What? That's what I meant to do!"

Louise named him Ti-Nou after a cousin of hers who grew up on the farm with her. He was born so-called mongoloid, which meant he couldn't go to school, but he willingly and enthusiastically participated in the daily chores. As he helped the men repair harnesses and build furniture, he learned a variety of manual skills and pretty soon was creating all kinds of original inventions of his own. I'm guessing that, when he was born, the doctors offered stern advice to the parents, words similar in tone to those of my vet, and the parents' reaction was identical to my own.

Masha, our Australian shepherd dog, licked that cat every way from Sunday, and when next spring came around, Ti-Nou was ready to go outside and explore and play, and he did that for ten wonderful years.

He learned to jump and run by keeping his back legs together and using them as a single limb, and even though he stayed close to the house and followed the other animals for safety, he became quite agile.

In his last week he stumbled on the basement steps and banged his head on the concrete basement floor. He died a few hours later from a cerebral concussion, precisely the prediction of the veterinarian who had first held him in his hands, ten years prior. Louise held him in her arms until he exhaled his last purr, and that was it.

Ten years. The vet's prognosis was accurate: the animal would eventually stumble and fall and fatally injure itself. That happened, exactly as predicted. Except that it happened ten years after it was supposed to.

The intervening years were pure joy for all of us, not the least of all for the cat.

He died on Tuesday, November 6th, the day of the US primaries, and we will never ever know who he voted for. Louise had laid his body out in state on the front porch, right in front of the door, wrapped in a ceremonial bath towel, so that I could stumble over him when I got home from work.

You have to bury him now.

Well, no.

Why not?

Because it's seven PM, it's pitch black outside, I'm cold, I'm tired, I'm hungry and I have to get up at six AM tomorrow morning. The cat can wait until the weekend.

What will we do with him in the meantime?

Put him in a plastic garbage bag and lay him to rest in the basement freezer, along with the rest of the meat. Think of it as the pussy morgue.

Eww! (Typical female reaction). We keep our food there!

Yup. And we do that to keep it from being infested with worms and disease. So that's where the cat is going, until I can give it a proper funeral, four days from now. It's that, or the dumpster.

Next garbage pick-up is on the coming Tuesday.

Saturday morning, mid-November. The ground is lightly covered with snow, but it hasn't completely frozen over yet. So, after breakfast I start to dig.

The thing with digging is, like so many other things in life, it's really hard to get started. The top six inches are tangled with roots and grass and weeds, and you feel as though it will never end. But once you get past that, the rest of the soil is loose and soft, and aside from a few large stones, the going is good, and you get a decent hole in no time.

So, I laid Ti-Nou to rest in a decent hole in the garden, wrapped in his bath-towel shroud. But now he needs a memorial.

I am not about to buy him a carved headstone, but I have other resources.

Almost one year ago to the day, I had dug up three small cherry trees from my front lawn.

All of them were children of a mature cherry tree that Louise had salvaged from a compost heap behind a garden center eight years before. Whether they grew from seeds that had fallen from the parent tree or emerged from its roots, I never knew. But there was one that was so pathetically tiny and warped that I never expected it to survive. In fact, the only reason that all three of the new shoots grew up to be little trees is because I never actually mow my lawn.

Part of the reason is that I am lazy. The other reason is that you would be astonished at what will spontaneously grow on your lawn if you don't cut it. I got three cherry trees, among other things.

So, I potted them and moved them to the back of the house, and then started to think about where I could plant them. I had all winter to do that. (Think about it, not actually do it.)

The next spring, the two bigger trees sprouted leaves and immediately began to behave like real plants. The runt, however, was recalcitrant. The entire upper half of its skinny, twisted trunk had dried up and rotted away like chaff, and none of the buds showed any signs of life. But I left it there, not because I was hopeful of a favourable outcome, but because, as I said, I am lazy. That big pot of wet soil is heavy. It can stay there for fifty years; I don't care. I'm not gonna bust a gut to move it somewhere else.

So, spring sprang, and summer ensued, and one day I noticed something.

That skinny, warped trunk had produced a single leaf. It was about the size of a match head, and close to the ground. Gna. Whatever. Good luck with that.

By August, that spindly little runt had surrounded itself with new growth and was easily competing with its larger cousins. The stunted, corkscrew trunk had grown back straight and true and even began to proffer new branches. It was still barely higher than my chin, but it seemed to be on a divine mission.

So, I thought, what better marriage than a handicapped resuscitated tree to celebrate the life and death of a handicapped rescue cat? The nutrients from the dead cat will feed the roots of the living tree, the cat will be remembered as long as the tree will grow, and I only have to dig one hole.

So be it. But I was in for another surprise.

The runty tree had spent a year in the twenty-litre pot that I had planted it in. At that time, the extent of its root system could be measured in inches.

When I turned over the pot to plant the tree over my cat, there was almost no more soil, only roots. A Medusa's head of thick, healthy roots all curled and wound about themselves within the confines of the pot like a nest of finger-thick white snakes. The root ball outweighed the visible part of the tree by at least twenty to one. That little bugger had been very busy underground, where no one but the worms could see.

So, the next time you come to see me and I offer you a sweet, ripe cherry from one of my trees, say a little prayer for Ti-Nou, the crazy cat who couldn't even scratch his own ears without tumbling over and spinning around like a duckpin.

"From my rotting body, flowers shall grow and I am in them, and that is eternity."

—Edvard Munch

BUGS

I LIKE BUGS.

Saturday morning, August 4th, 2018.

Dave! Come quick! There's a bug eating my parsley! Louise, my wife, is clearly agitated.

I abandon my newspaper and coffee and investigate.

Sure enough, there's a giant shiny black and yellow caterpillar diligently munching away at the parsley plant in front of my house. It looks both toxic and goofy, and it is totally oblivious to my presence. It's about the size of my pinkie, which is pretty big for a bug. I can hear it chewing.

I squint at it and say, "Yup. He's eating your parsley all right," then return to my typical Saturday morning activities. Coffee and a crossword puzzle.

Louise is irritated; at the bug, and at me.

"You have to get rid of it!" she shouts.

OK then. But before we get too hasty, don't you want to know what the hell it is?

So, I google it. "Black and yellow caterpillar." And there it is. A black swallowtail butterfly larva. I show the pictures to my wife.

So, should I just squish it under my shoe, or can I feed it to one of the chickens?

When she saw the pictures of the butterfly that it would become, she softened her tone.

"OK. He can eat all of my parsley. I don't care. But how does it become a butterfly?"

We googled that too. Apparently when they are stuffed to the gills with parsley, they trundle off to some other place and attach themselves to a small branch somewhere and then … become something else.

Sunday morning, August 5th, 2018.

Louise typically wakes up at 4:30 or 5 AM; I prefer to sleep in until at least 6. But that morning, Louise dragged me out of bed and wailed, "The bug is on the move! He's left the parsley plant! He's stomping around the edge of the pot!"

Stomping. I can almost hear his multiple pairs of hobnailed Bovva boots clanging against the rim of the plastic pot.

I can understand her concern. The bug is looking for a branch, and the nearest tree is forty feet away. He's not gonna make it. Not a chance in hell.

OK then. I pull on a pair of shorts and go outside. I find a ten-litre food-grade bucket, cut up a handful of small branches and stuff them in the bucket, then put the bug in the bucket. I cut a thin piece of plywood into a doughnut shape, then raid the kitchen cupboards for a plastic colander about the same diameter as the bucket.

Bucket, plywood doughnut and upside-down plastic colander get all wired together to create an impromptu vivarium for the bug, and the whole mess gets parked on a chair on the gallery right outside of my front door, in the shade and protected from the wind and rain.

Monday morning, August 6th, 2018.

The bug, after exploring every single centimetre of its new environment, has chosen a branch to anchor itself to. It has woven a loop of silken string that supports its upper body and cemented its butt permanently to the bottom of the branch. I have serious misgivings about my decision to constrain the bug to an environment that I have contrived for it, rather than allowing it to live out its life naturally.

Wednesday morning, August 8th, 2018.

The bug has shrunken slightly in size, the skin is beginning to wrinkle and the bright yellow-green colouring is fading to dark grey. It has been exceptionally hot and dry, and I suspect that the larva has desiccated and died.

Saturday morning, August 11th, 2018.

The larva has shrunk to a fraction of its original size. It is a cold, hard, shrivelled-up little piece of dross, black as coal and indistinguishable from the dead branches that constitute its environment. It actually looks like a tiny black piece of dried-up dogshit. Louise is convinced that it is quite dead, and that it should be relegated to the compost heap. I share her sentiments, based on the physical evidence, but my glass is always half full, and I'm lazy, so I wait.

Monday evening, August 13th, 2018.

I get home from work about 6 PM. My improvised vivarium is no longer on the chair in front of the door. Louise has dumped it on my work table in the garden.

"Your bug is dead," she said. "Nothing living will ever emerge from that bucket."

Out of sympathy for the dead bug, I took the bucket, like a last resting place, and put it in a more comfortable spot, in the shade of a wood pile, in the open air. I felt personally responsible for the death of my bug. How arrogant of me to think that I knew better than mother nature.

Wednesday, August 15th, 2018.

After almost a month of blistering hot temperatures and almost no rain, we had what can be politely called a shitstorm. Blustering winds and rain like you can't believe.

Thursday, August 16th, 2018.

I got home from work at about 6 PM, thoroughly exhausted. Louise was working late, so I was all alone. Usually I would have a quick snack and then go out and work for a while outside, but that evening I decided to go and lie down for a bit.

About eight o'clock I woke up with a start. Something was wrong.

Usually, when something is wrong, the dog barks or the chicken mafia cluck en masse in front of the door or the duck wakes up the entire neighbourhood. But this time it was the total silence that jerked me suddenly from my somnolescent reverie.

I got up, put on some shorts, and went outside. I noticed that my improvised vivarium had taken on some water, and that my little pile of sticks had all tumbled to the bottom. I plucked off the colander lid and sifted through the soaked debris, one stick at a time, in search of the remains of my bug.

When I found it, I was astonished. All that remained was a thin, empty, chitin skin with a tiny slit along the abdomen. The bug had escaped!

But there was no way that The Bug could have fled the wired-up container, and there was no evidence of The Bug inside.

Then I flipped over the lid. And there it was. The most beautiful butterfly that you have ever seen. It was completely immobile, with the wings upright and tightly pressed together.

I poked it gently with one finger, but got no response. I waited a moment, then gently pressed my finger under its front legs. It slowly and reluctantly climbed onto the tip of my index, clinging tightly to the skin with its tiny claws, then seemed to go back into a coma.

I walked it about for a few minutes, pointing it this way and that, but it might just as well have been a tiny, ephemeral origami paper ornament. So, I parked it on a sunflower, and it again reluctantly and mechanically stepped onto its new perch, where it stayed immobile for at least an hour.

When it finally flew away, I was elated. I felt as though I, too, had just grown paper-thin imaginary wings and had been swept aloft by a soft, warm, flower-scented summer breeze.

LEAVES

I LIKE LEAVES.

Leaves are wonderful things. While they are on the tree, they look great, and the tree is very happy. When they begin to fall, though, strange shit happens.

I don't rake leaves. My neighbours rake them frantically, fanatically and constantly, as if their mere presence will kill them. As if they were toxic waste. They rake and bag and rake and bag, and use gas-powered leaf-blowers to kettle the poor bastards before they can escape. Often, they will step out after supper with a flashlight to hand-pick the few strays that fell or got blown in since the last frenetic capture one hour ago. It's almost a paramilitary operation.

And every Tuesday, garbage day, from late September until almost Christmas, I run the gauntlet of walls of green, black and orange polythene bags filled with dead leaves on both sides of the street, waiting for the garbage truck to haul them away to dead-leaf plastic-bag landfill heaven.

My dead leaves are not toxic waste. They are a precious resource.

In the spring, the few that have not already mulched back into the ground are hiding in little corners where the wind swept them. If they're in the shade, they are damp and soggy and smell like mould, and they're full of tiny earthworms. If they are in a sunny place, they are crunchy and dry and they smell like spring, and spiders.

So last Saturday was still winter. The thermometer said eight degrees, but the blistering north wind cancelled that out and it was still winter. Then the next day, Sunday, it was twenty-two degrees in the shade and, presto, it was spring, as if someone had pulled a switch, after four months of constant, piercing cold.

So, I went out and scraped up a tiny pile of dead leaves, vestiges of last fall's holocaust.

Within minutes my cat had decided to take up residency; this was HIS pile of leaves. He settled in, comfy-cozy, and began to nod off.

A few minutes later, the Chicken Mafia got wind of the leaf pile. They showed up in force and confronted the cat.

"Step away from the leaves, cat, if you know what's good for you! We'll take over from here."

"Screw you, stoopid chickens. I was here first. Go get yer own leaves!"

The hens clucked among themselves for a moment, bemusedly. The cat clearly did not understand the basic rules.

"Listen, cat, and listen good," clucked the chicken matriarch. "Every single leaf on this territory belongs to us. Bar none. No exceptions. You can go chase your mice and birds and do whatever other disgusting stuff that you like, that's your business. You can climb trees and scratch and poop wherever you want whenever you want, and that's OK. But you touch one more of our leaves and you are dog meat. Are we clear?"

The other chickens all clucked in unanimous consent.

"Cheese. Lighten up a bit. It's not like there's a shortage of leaves."

The chicken laid her beady eye on the cat.

"The leaves are MINE. All of them. If you wish to fight for them, we will."

By this time the cat was surrounded by fourteen angry chickens and two irate ducks. He wisely beat a hasty retreat.

Four minutes later the Chicken Mafia had scratched and pecked the entire leaf pile to mulch and moved on to other chickenesque preoccupations. The cat came back to the house and consoled itself with a bowl of kibble and a nap on the couch.

The moral here? Don't fuck with a gaggle of angry chickens in commando mode!

TREES

I LIKE TREES.

I prefer them when they are alive, but this one was quite obviously dead. For three years it had sat in a pot at the front of the property, and for the first two years it had more or less prospered. But this spring, after the winter melt, the entire tree except for a few sprigs on the few remaining bottom branches was totally, definitively, stone-cold dead.

The upper trunk and the upper branches snapped off in my fingers like bone-dry match sticks. I grabbed the three-foot high trunk at the base and carried it to the compost heap, where I shook the tree out from its container, and tossed it onto the pile.

I came back four days later with a pair of rose cutters, intent on reducing the remains of that tree to compost. After four days in the blazing sun, with roots exposed, it should have been dry enough to shred into flakes.

I grasped the trunk with my left hand and began snipping the tree into pieces, starting from the top and moving down towards the seared roots. I was halfway through before I noticed two remarkable things.

The first thing was an overpowering smell of balsam. That made me look closer at the object in my hand.

The second thing was two tiny little lime-green buds at the base of the trunk, smaller than a match-head but as alive as you and I. Shit. The fucking tree is still alive. And I'm chopping it up for sausage meat. I've already sliced off almost three-quarters of it; there's only a tiny stump left.

So, I dump the exfoliated remains back into the pot from which it had emerged, refill it with a few spadefuls of soil, and drench the whole stew with a dollop of rain water from a nearby bucket. Then I park the mess in a quiet spot in the shade. I sit down in the grass right next to the victim, and light up a smoke.

"I'm so sorry," I said. "I really honestly thought that you were dead."

The tree did not respond. At least, not immediately.

I sat there with my remorse and my cigarette, and then the tree spoke.

Not loudly, like you and I, but tree-like, the way they whisper amongst themselves when the wind is high.

"Thank you," the little tree said.

FENCES

I LIKE FENCES.

Good ones are supposed to make good neighbours, but can bad neighbours build good fences?

Here's a silly story about one particular fence.

Once upon a time I had good relations with my neighbour. We helped each other out with simple home repairs, lent each other tools, even shared some meals or a few beers on a hot summer day.

But somehow, for no particular reason, the relationship went sour. Arguments arose about whose dog pooped on whose lawn, or if the wind shifted left or right, who got the dandelion seeds or the dead leaves from the other guy's lawn. He also seriously objected to my chickens.

"We're not in the country here!" he shouted at me from his side. That was funny, because the next property to the south of ours is a cow pasture. Inhabited by real cows. I can see them from my kitchen window, just the other side of the fence, and so can he. Beyond that is the tree-lined river, and on the other side is a corn field that stretches to the horizon, and in the autumn the wild deer migrate up from there to eat the apples straight off my tree, thirty feet from the house.

So, the neighbour, at great expense to himself, decided to erect a fence between us. It was a very nice fence, a Frost fence about five feet high, with steel posts on concrete footings every eight feet.

He did all of the work himself, and he was damned proud of that fence.

They say that good fences make good neighbours, but in this case the fence was merely palliative. Good fences cannot compensate for bad intentions.

The problem was that the fence was erected in the summer. When winter came, he suddenly realized that he could no longer just plow the snow from his driveway directly on to my property, which incidentally is illegal and which he had allowed himself to do without my permission ever since before I even bought the place. Now there was a brand-new, self-erected expensive fence in the way.

My problem was that the people who had built my house some fifty years prior had decided to do so at the lowest part of the property, ensuring that with every spring melt they could enjoy Niagara Falls in the privacy of their own basement. So, I figured with the new fence in the way, the neighbour would plow his excess snow elsewhere, and I would have a bit less water in the basement next spring.

His problem was that putting the snow somewhere else meant filling up a trailer and hauling it down to the bottom of his property, some hundred yards away. Clearing his driveway suddenly took three hours, instead of thirty minutes. Bummer.

So, he took on a new tactic. Instead of shooting his snow horizontally onto my property, as he did in pre-fence days, he shot it vertically over the fence. Problem solved.

Well, his problem maybe. My problem was that the new snow, instead of being spread out over a certain area, was piling up dramatically on my side of the fence, where I had recently planted some young trees.

So, I called the cops. They came, they warned him that he can't blow his snow either onto the public road or onto a neighbour's property. But don't call us back for this bullshit, we have other fish to fry.

The next snowfall, it was business as usual. He's out there, blowing his snow over the fence on to my side. So, I go and talk to him. He gives me the finger and aims his snow plow directly at my face. Under those circumstances, I have to resign. I have lost this battle. He will continue to dump his snow on my property and I am powerless to prevent him.

And so it went for two years. I spent time and money to excavate around the house, putting in drains and banking the soil to control spring run off, and planting trees near the property line to limit erosion. The neighbour continued each winter to sling his excess snow over his fence onto my side, thumbing his nose at me and knowing full well that there was absolutely nothing that I could do about it.

Here's the funny part. This year we had an exceptionally huge snowfall, with heavy wet snow and rain and ice. The neighbour had plowed so much of that abundance onto my side that his beautiful brand-new ten-thousand-dollar stainless steel fence with concrete footings looks today as if it had been hit by mortar shells. It just couldn't withstand the weight of the snow and ice that he had piled on top of it.

On my side, I had planted hardy, gutsy trees. Not hundred-dollar designer shrubs, but blood-and-guts saplings rooted out from the native forest. After being crushed down as hard as the fence, they just sprang back as if nothing had ever happened. The precious fence, however, is a total write-off.

BURRITOS AND MIRACLES

I LIKE BURRITOS.

One ingredient is guacamole.

Mooshed up, overripe avocados. Throw some garlic and onions in there and dive in! DELICIOUS! Avocados used to be called Alligator Pears. Until they actually changed the name, not very many people actually wanted to eat them.

I ate a burrito once. It came from a Canadian fast-food chain specialized in Mexican food.

That's a bit funny, because when I travelled in Mexico back in 1988, nobody had ever heard of a burrito, much less a taco. Including the native Mexicans, unless you were a tourist hanging out in the tourist spots.

While travelling I jumped the fence and drove around in a rented jeep. Not a nice new Cherokee or a Wrangler, with AM/FM radio, power windows and air conditioning. It was US Army surplus left over from the Korean war, complete with a bullet-proof steel plate floor and solid hardwood seats and no top or sides or seat belts, just a fold-down plexiglass windshield that came up to my nose and a solid steel stick shift that went from the floor to my chin and required both fists to manipulate. I could imagine Major General Douglas MacArthur himself riding shotgun with his aviator glasses and corncob pipe, barrelling through the frozen mud at Inchon, dodging Chinese bullets as he barked out orders to the troops.

My ride was almost as comfortable as his must have been.

I spent time in coastal villages that were deprived of running water, electricity, public transport, cars, and telephones. Most people lived in shelters cobbled together from salvaged driftwood and discarded auto parts, sleeping in suspended hammocks to stay above the moist, insect-ridden beaten earth floor.

But they had food. Not abundant or luxurious, but delicious and sustaining. It kept you on your feet, and reminded you why it was good to be alive.

The kinds of meals that they served up were almost identical to the type that you would serve to your own children. A plate with a small portion of animal protein, either fresh-caught fish or barnyard fowl or some remnant of a mammalian ruminant, and sometimes road kill (I was once offered fried armadillo), accompanied by a dollop of a stew of rice and beans and vegetables. And a thin slice of corn bread (the taco) to mop up the mess afterwards.

And they were really fond of french fries. Even the most remote, isolated and underprivileged communities always had french fries. They may have cooked them up in used crankcase oil, but they were a staple.

That was real Mexican food. That was what real Mexicans ate. Not tacos, or burritos, or enchiladas.

The first time that I ever ate a burrito was in Laval, a prosperous middle-class suburb north of Montreal, in 2015. I had to meet a client in a popular shopping center on a Saturday morning, and invited my wife, Louise, to accompany me. By noon we had conducted our business, and we were both a bit hungry. Since we were in a suburban shopping mall, exactly nine stores out of twelve were actually restaurants. I have never ever understood the logic behind that.

Louise lusted for pizza or poutine or fried chicken, and I was fed up with Sushi, so I just gave her twenty bucks and told her to go eat whatever she wanted. Then I gravitated towards the Mexican fast food place.

I didn't recognize anything on the menu, so I humbly asked the attendant do guide me.

"Dude, you need a BURRITO!" he promptly replied. The pimply-faced kid looked and sounded about as Mexican as I did. But his youthful enthusiasm seduced me, and since he worked there, he obviously knew a whole lot more about the vast array of ingredients on his side of the counter than I did. And so I complied.

The thing was the size and shape of a fucking football, and it contained black beans, brown rice, meat, guacamole, sauce, corn, cheese, lettuce, tomatoes, onions, cilantro, yogurt and sour cream and more sauce, and it was FUCKING delicious except that I could only eat about one-third of it. Still, I was hooked. No more McDonald's or Wendy's or Harvey's for me; if ever I get a hankering for fast food, it will be a BURRITO.

That was several years ago. Yesterday, I got the call, from the bottom of my pathetic, sinful soul. I needed a burrito. I ordered the smallest one that they have, which they call "regular," but even so it was twice as much food than I can actually eat all at once. The renowned cartoonist Bernard Kliban once advised to never eat anything bigger than your head, and I have followed his sound wisdom for most of my life.

That was Saturday. When I got home, I guiltily tossed the rest of my meal on the ground, and my chickens greedily gobbled up the sloppy mess that was once a noble pseudo-Latino sandwich. Within seconds, not an iota of my leftover meal was to be seen, not even the tiny cubes of crispy spicy chicken.

And yes, chickens actually eat, um, chicken. There would be a moral dilemma here unless you realize that chickens will, in fact, eat and digest absolutely anything and everything, including rocks. OK, small ones and not that many all at once, but still, rocks. Remember the raptors from "Jurassic Park"? Chickens are just really very small raptors.

The next morning, Sunday, I got up early to do some yard work. By noon, my wife Louise suggested a snack. "How about a plain omelette with some cheese and toast?"

OK. So, she hauls out three fist-sized eggs from underneath our dear chickens, still body-warm. The eggs are so large that we can't close the cartons, and she has to crack them three or four times against the side of the bowl in order to break the thick, hard, brown shells. The yolks are the size of golf balls and the colour of sunflowers, and the liquid inside is as thick and sticky as warm honey.

Ten minutes later, I am merely staring at my plate.

"What, you're not hungry?" she asks.

"Oh, I'm hungry all right. I'm just contemplating a miracle."

"What miracle?"

Twenty hours ago, that omelet was a discarded burrito.

SITTING ON THE HUMP

I LIKE CHRISTINE.

She's a woman I accidentally met in Saint-Jerome who was willing to sell her body for a pack of smokes. Or maybe even for a single cigarette.

But not just to anybody. She had her principles.

Her name was Christine and the only reason that I remember it is because it's the same name as the murderous car in the Steven King novel that healed itself. (The car, not the novel.)

It's funny because she would drop her shorts for a few dollars, but not with anyone. Just with people who shared her traditional values.

"Kids today," she would say, "they're fucking each other up the ass, gangbanging each other. They don't even know how to have normal sex. The girls are shaving their assholes and paying to get them bleached and the boys are botoxing their testicles. It's totally perverse."

This is coming from a semi-professional prostitute, and also a grandmother. She was fifty years old when she confessed those words to me. I eventually met her daughter and her two grandchildren, and she spoke to me about her father who was withering away in a hospital in Montreal from some unspecified disease. That's four generations.

At fifty, Christine was still physically desirable, but it was obvious that she wanted to retire, although towards what, or from what, nobody could tell, not even her.

She was lucky, or smart, or both. Most women in her profession are stone cold dead by the time they get to her age.

I always went to great lengths to remember as little about her as I could, out of respect for her desire for anonymity. I knew which street she lived on, but I refused to remember the name. It was likewise for the civic address and the apartment number. It was the first building after the second stop sign on the right, and the buzzer for her apartment was the third from the bottom. I only knew her age because she made a big brouhaha about turning fifty, and I get that; surviving the first half-century is memorable for anyone.

But it was more information than I needed, or wanted. I knew damn well how old she was, give or take a few years, but as long as it was speculative she could have been any age at all. She could giggle like a teenager, but she knew all the words by heart to the songs on the radio from forty years ago. Having her age confirmed was like opening Schrödinger's box, and I felt as if the cat had long ago expired.

I also accidentally learned her last name, because once she made a pun on it. It was a good joke, but I won't repeat it.

I also learned that she used to be a carpenter until a car accident smashed her lower body to pieces and after years of operations she became addicted to Oxycontin and welfare. Her legs and hips were smothered in scars from the accident and from the endless operations, her bones were bolted together with a ton of titanium, and she eventually just slid down between the cracks in the floor, where she ultimately found rest and peace.

I saw her legs once. She wanted to change her pants before I drove her to the dollar store, and since she lived in a one-room basement apartment there was no place to hide. She modestly asked me not to peek, so being the gentleman that I am, I did. I peeked.

To quote Bugs Bunny in "The Rabbit of Seville," she looked as if she had been through a machine. Although she still had a pretty decent butt, for a girl her age.

She would often chastise me because I would casually toss my cigarette butts out of my car window. "Can you PLEASE help so that my grandchildren will have a fucking decent planet to grow up in!?" She would stab me in the sternum with a stern, stiff pointy index finger. Once, she actually slapped my face, like Scarlett O'Hara, because I had extinguished a live butt under my toe on the sidewalk.

Another time she asked me to take her "special" shopping. (I.e., somewhere other than the dollar store.) "I really need goat cheese and garlic crackers," she explained. Women are so strange; even today I don't get it at all.

OK. But let me clarify. We're not talking about a penthouse escort. We're talking about an ordinary woman who is a grandmother and who lives in a basement tenement welfare bachelor apartment and who uses dollar-store dishwashing liquid to wash her hair and her underwear and her dishes, often simultaneously, and who sucks dick for extra cash or just to overcome her boredom and remind her that she used to be desirable and seductive and allows her to knit out a fragile social network that partially and temporarily justifies her own microscopically tiny sacred place in the universe.

She dragged me to *Les Étals*, an upper-crust import emporium, and implored me to wait for her in the parking lot while she spent her own money (aside from the loose change that she scraped off of the dashboard of my car without my consent) on crackers and cheese. She had to count out nickels and dimes at the cash to pay for it. I sat there, the engine turned off, but not silent at all.

To my right, on the street, the traffic whizzed noisily back and forth. Massive diesel-powered delivery trucks trundled shiploads of stuff either way, and the smell and sound and the vibration of the pavement that they produced was enough to keep you awake and alert and mildly ill. To my left, a cleft of old trees harboured a loud gaggle of chirping birds and chattering squirrels. The smell of diesel exhaust from the trucks barreling up and down the road blended exotically with the scent of wild flowers that sprang spontaneously from the cracks in the asphalt at the edge of the paved lot, and wild bees and butterflies lazily buzzed and flittered over the sparse weeds that clung to the edge of the hot bitumen.

After a few minutes Christine emerged with her treasure. She parked her shapely but gradually and inevitably aging ass in the passenger seat and asked, "You got a knife?"

I'm sitting in the driver's seat of my car, in the hard, hot blacktop parking lot of the shop. I am bereft of appropriate cutlery. The only hardware that I can produce is a tiny pocket knife that I use to scrape the daily filth from under my fingernails. I hand it to her.

Christine busts open her packages like a child on Christmas day. She uses the tiny, filthy knife and her equally unhygienic fingers to smoosh a wad of goat cheese onto a dry garlic-flavoured cracker. "Here!" she shoves the impromptu snack into my face, and provocatively licks her dirty, sticky digits.

It was truly delicious. The marriage of flavours and textures was quite extraordinary. A glass of Chardonnay would have been totally appropriate, except that we were sitting in a car on a hot asphalt parking lot in the middle of nowhere.

Then Christine turned to me and said something quite extraordinary.

"You know, Dave, you and I, we are very lucky."

Why? I thought. Because you are wiping your greasy diseased cheese-laden fingers on the seat of my car and brushing the garlic cracker crumbs clinging to your generous but gradually wrinkling cleavage onto the floor mat? I don't really mind; a smile from a pretty woman, no matter how insincere, can melt an old man's heart like so much candle wax. And don't they know it!

Then she confessed her secret.

"You and I, and everyone our age, we are living in a very special time. We grew up knowing animals and birds and trees and nature and stuff, and almost no technology. The next generation after us will be exactly the opposite. They'll never see a tree or a squirrel or a bird or a blade of grass, but they'll be born with a smart phone up their ass. You and I, we're sitting on the hump."

I thought about that for a minute while Christine wadded up another toxic cracker-and-cheese combo. Me sitting on the hump in my crumb-dusted, cheese-greased car in a parking lot eating crackers and cheese with a two-bit worm-eaten fifty-cent over-the-hill whore from nowhere, who washes her hair and her panties and her dishes with dollar-store soap, but who owned a shitload of impromptu philosophy.

We are sitting on the hump. Those were her exact verbatim words.

The last time I went to visit Christine, I drove along the street whose name I don't remember, parked in front of the building whose address I ignore, and poked the buzzer to the apartment number that I never knew. There was no answer. I have never seen her since.

But ever since then I have never ever stopped sitting on the hump.

CHICKEN SOUP

The Chicken was smaller than all of the other chickens in the coop, and regularly got beat up and bullied and injured by the others, so that we had to adopt her inside the house.

The Chicken follows Tantie Weeze (my niece's name for my wife) absolutely everywhere. When Louise goes to the kitchen, it's to make food, and The Chicken wants some. Not because The Chicken is particularly hungry, although they always are, but just because The Chicken wants to be included in whatever is going on. It considers itself as part of the family, and is not shy to express its opinion.

Kinda like a puppy dog.

And that damned chicken has a vocabulary that would shame a grade-schooler. It purrs, it clucks, it crows and clicks and growls and produces a host of other noises that surpass the imagination. Research has shown that chickens invent names to describe individual people and other animals in their entourage, and they use them to gossip about us behind our backs. No joke.

I called The Chicken "Chicken Soup," because, when Louise was making some, The Chicken wanted some too. I was the only one in the house who saw the irony.

Except maybe the cat. He's smarter than he looks, and more sophisticated than he behaves, but he has some serious, unresolved issues with chickens. He's supposed to be the predator, and they the prey, but in reality, it works out the other way, and that seriously undermines his self-esteem.

Louise calls The Chicken Poopie, because it poops. Little, dry, dime-sized poops, but still, chicken poop. She also calls it Poopie because it sounds like "Puppy" which was Louise's pet name for Masha, our Australian Shepherd dog who died recently, and who was our precious companion for thirteen years.

The little chicken produces about four or five tiny chicken poops a day. Louise scoops them up as we go, but for anyone who wants to adopt a chicken, you can buy chicken diapers that are custom-made and adjustable and machine-washable. They've got elastic bands and Velcro straps that will comfortably suit any chicken.

I kid you not. It's a global feminist grass-roots thing; teaching Philippine girls to sew and generating revenues for poor women in the third world. They cost about twenty bucks, and are made entirely from recycled materials. (I.e., some gurlz gotta dumpster dive.) Or maybe it's just selvage from garment sweat shops. I dunno.

Just google it. Chicken diapers. It's a thing. No kidding.

The Chicken follows Louise absolutely everywhere, just like a poopy puppy, even to the bathroom, and talks non-stop. It wants to be picked up and petted like a dog and it will tell you its entire life story in a random and disparate series of chicken noises that only Louise can understand.

Yesterday The Chicken pulled a ceramic tile off the kitchen floor and scratched out the entire space underneath, right down to the plywood, and actually ate most of the filth that it found under there.

Meanwhile, the chicken coop outside is frozen in. We can't open the door; the bottom is seized up in eighteen inches of solid ice, hard as concrete. So, Louise pushed out one of the plastic window panes so that she could feed and water them through the hole. On the weekend I will have to unhinge the door and saw it in half so that we will be able to open the top part but leave the bottom part as a barrier, because otherwise when that shit starts melting the chickens will drown. Or I'll have to move them ALL into the house.

I don't mind, except that these are very territorial animals. I may have to sleep on the couch, or even on the floor.

I haven't seen this much snow since 1971.

So. Chicken coops, chicken soups, chicken poops. That's a chicken – OOPS – rhyme/scan trifecta. Do I win a prize? (It's actually a quadrifecta, if such a beast exists, if you simply include the word OOPS, which is really appropriate in all of the other three cases.)

So, yeah. The Chicken poops all over the place. As long as it happens on the hard floor, it's not a problem.

But now the chicken wants to sleep with us in our bed. They are very social animals, like I said. We need chicken diapers.

As mentioned, if you google "chicken diapers," there are a number of proposed solutions. There are the hand-stitched designer models that cost twenty bucks a throw, or there are instructions on how to make one yourself from an old sock.

Or you can buy a pack of particle masks from Walmart and strap one of them onto your chicken's butt hole. Five bucks gets you twenty chicken diapers, and they work like a charm.

So, I went to Walmart to buy some chicken diapers. Except that I couldn't find them. It's a big store with a lot of products, and if you just wander randomly through the aisles you will surely die long before you ever find what you are looking for.

So, I went to the counter, which was well served by two very young genteel ladies. Obviously, I did not ask them for chicken diapers. I asked for particle masks.

These events were all pre-Covid, when most people (including me) couldn't tell their masks from their elbows, and the things cost about a quarter each. But these two innocent young things were really on the ball.

"They're right behind you. What size do you need?"

Say what? they come in different sizes!?

"We have adult and children's sizes. Who are they for?"

Shit. The gig is up; I am so busted. I am like Honest Abe Lincoln; I cannot tell a lie.

"It's for my chicken."

The two young ladies looked at me as if I had just dropped my shorts and laid an egg. I'm pretty sure that the senior one, who was, like, seventeen, was trained to call security in cases like mine, and I am convinced that she was about to do so.

I had to act fast. "My chicken is injured. We are treating it in the house. I need diapers to prevent it from pooping all over the place."

Blank stares, stiff white lips. A tiny bead of sweat on their foreheads. A nervous trigger-finger twitching over the "call security" button like Wyatt Earp at the OK Corral.

"I saw it on Youtube."

"Oh. If you saw it on Youtube, it must be God's own truth. Here you go! Have a nice day!"

I love millennials. Clueless and fragile, but with hearts of gold, and a helluva lot smarter than they look.

And now I know how they feel about old farts like me who want to buy chicken diapers.

GOT SKUNKS?

I've got three. Twenty feet from the front door. They have dug themselves a nice comfy nest under the barn and they adore Louise's home-cooked leftovers.

As long as they stay out there, they are wildlife.

My cat and my chickens have no argument with them; nor do I. They have all established their own pecking order out on the terrain, and I do not interfere.

I might regret this later on, but for now everyone seems to agree on who gets first dibs on the open buffet of spaghetti Bolognese au gratin in rain water sauce with a side of stale bread and wilted salad.

This is not vermin. They eat the unripe, bug-riddled apples that fall out of my tree. They devour the potato peels that I throw onto my compost, and they vigorously dig for the fat white underground slugs that will all conspire to destroy my cherry tree next spring.

This is their land, not mine. I am the interloper, the intruder, the destroyer.

I would prefer to be remembered as the protector, the guardian, the nurturer.

People don't like skunks because they stink.

Word up, people. They only stink when you make them angry. If you don't annoy them, they are as docile as kittens. You can train them to eat out of your hand.

Just don't let them inside the house. Then they are vermin, and you need a professional exterminator. Most people would either laugh at me or regard me as a bit daffy, but maybe my tolerance for skunks was acquired at a tender young age.

Anyone who was a child in the Sixties grew up on *Looney Tunes* cartoons. A black-and-white TV with rabbit-ear antennas and four channels, and on Saturday morning you got to watch Bugs Bunny, Elmer Fudd, Sylvester the Cat, Tweety Bird, Foghorn Leghorn, and Yosemite Sam (The rootin'est, shootin'est, KAYootinest hombre west, south, north AND east of the Pecos!) resolve a variety of mutual conflicts using an astonishing array of stylized acts of extreme violence.

But the skunk Pepe le Pew takes the cake. He is a caricature of Maurice Chevalier or possibly Yves Montand, or maybe even Charles Boyer, all of whom were male sex idols of contemporary French cinema and all were type-cast hard-core ladies' men.

Pepe is one of the most obnoxious and dangerous sexual predators that has ever existed. If I had to present a video conference to men on how not to behave toward the gentler sex, I would just show them a Pepe le Pew cartoon. If Pepe were alive today, he would be serving a lifetime jail sentence for sexual harassment, stalking, groping, public indecency and the list goes on. That skunk does not understand the meaning of consent.

("My hobbee eez makingue LOOOVE!")

OK then. To be fair, by modern standards, every single character in the *Looney Tunes* repertoire, including Daffy Duck, Tweety Bird, Speedy Gonzales, the Coyote and the Road Runner all have the criminal profiles of violent psychopathic serial killers. Public enemy number one would be Bugs Bunny, the ultimate bad-ass foul-mouthed belligerent Yankee provocateur. But he looks SOO good in drag! (Are those B cups on that wascally wabbit or what!?) Gnyaaa, what's up doc?

Foghorn Leghorn is a decent runner-up for a serial killer profile. Gnyaaa, SHADDUP! Followed by baseball bat beatings, broken teeth, and black eyes. Wholesome cartoon entertainment for all ages, approved for young children. We ate it up!

So, yeah. As long as the skunks don't try to badger my cats, or move into my house, I'll continue to allow them to let me share their space.

A-ba-dee-a-ba-doo-abba-da; dat's all folks! (With a tip of the hat to Mel Blanc.)

Is that OK?

Well, no. Since I wrote this, the obnoxious skunk has in fact been expunged from the public record, along with numerous other favourite childhood cartoon characters that have been declared unsuitable for genteel viewers. Pepe has been accused, tried and condemned for promoting rape culture. I guess they finally established a clear and undeniable scientific link between a cartoon skunk drawn sixty years ago and the proliferation of sexual violence today.

Meanwhile, my favorite pick-up line will always be, "Come weez me to ze Casbah my darleeng! We weel make be-yooteeful muzique togezzer!"

It never worked, either for Pepe or myself, but it's fun to say.

FOOD

I LIKE VEGETABLES.

Don't get me wrong. I'm no vegan. That crackpot ideology is right up there with Hare Krishna and Scientology and Jim Jones and Zoroastrian fire worship.

I like meat too. I eat raw bacon and raw beef and I butter my toast (with real butter) before I toast it, so that the bread actually fries nice and crispy in the toaster, and if you leave a sliver of pork fat on your plate I will eat that too. My favourite dessert is sausage, but I will settle for cheese.

But vegetables are yummy and healthy and they just look and feel and smell so cool. And they contribute to the absolute best part of my day, sitting on the crapper at six AM with a cigarette and a crossword puzzle. It's like a prolonged daily orgasm.

I try to grow my own, but I live in Saint-Jerome, at the foot of the Laurentian mountains, so the soil is basically just sand and rocks. Mostly rocks.

Every year I spend a fortune on black earth and fertilizer and plants and seeds, and the total output for the entire season would fill a small bucket. This year I got a handful of peas, four or five string beans, three cucumbers and a bowlful of tomatoes.

So, around this time of year I head out to the farmer's market. It's an explosion of sensations, visual, auditory, olfactory, and social. Absolutely nothing is weighed or measured. The producers just eyeball it. A crate of tomatoes? Fill 'em up yea high. Pick the one you want; they're all the same price.

You want squash? Three bucks a pop, two for a fin, regardless of the type or size. There's no pocket change; everything is rounded out to the nearest dollar. And don't ask for a receipt. And you can't haggle, although the more you buy, the cheaper it gets.

Some weirdness always happens.

One woman showed up with a printed recipe. She wanted exactly forty-five tomatoes, no more, no less. Why exactly forty-five tomatoes? I didn't ask. Maybe she was making a giant tomato cake for her husband's forty-fifth.

The woman selling the tomatoes told her that the twenty-dollar crate held thirty tomatoes. How did she know that? Did she actually count every tomato that went into every single crate? Of course not. But she's been growing, harvesting and selling tomatoes since before she learned how to walk. Maybe there were only twenty-five tomatoes in that crate. Maybe there were thirty-four. It depends on the size of the tomato.

The client didn't want to buy two crates, because that was fifteen too many tomatoes, so she opted for one crate and two small baskets, for a total of about forty-eight tomatoes, and it cost her exactly the same price as two crates, or sixty tomatoes.

One young man wanted to buy garlic. He went to a stall and asked the seller if he had any. The old man limped over to his customer and pointed upwards, where an array of garlic tresses hung from a cord across the entire table, about twelve feet wide. The biggest one held eight bulbs and sold for fifteen bucks. The smallest one held two, and sold for five dollars, or two for nine.

How much for three? the client asked. The farmer answered, five bucks each, two for nine. He could have said, four-fifty each, but everything is rounded off to the nearest dollar. The young man bought three pairs for a total of fourteen dollars, or about $2.30 per bulb. For a dollar more, he could have bought eight bulbs instead of six, or $1.85 per bulb. Apparently, he doesn't know that you can hang those puppies from a nail on your kitchen wall and they will last for an entire year. If I bought just six bulbs of garlic, I would run out before the end of the week.

So, I splurged and bought exactly eighty-one dollars of fresh, farm-grown, sun-ripened, hand-picked vegetables, and counting what I bought last week, I probably have enough to keep me to Christmas (oops, sorry, the "Holiday Season") and beyond.

But before I did that, I had to withdraw some cash, because the farmers don't take plastic. There's an IGA grocery store on my way to the public market that has an ATM machine, so I stopped in there on my way. They had a huge display of jack-o'-lantern pumpkins in the parking lot, each about the size of a soccer ball, marked down from $4.99 to a mere $3.49. The farmers sell exactly the same ones for one dollar each. I could fill my car, including the trunk, the front and back seats, and the glove compartment for thirty bucks.

People buy those to decorate their front porches for Halloween and then throw them in the garbage the very next day because they don't realize that it is actually the main ingredient in pumpkin pie. What, precisely, do they think that pumpkin pies are made of? They would much rather discard the four-dollar fresh pumpkin and then buy a six-dollar can of pre-processed pumpkin pie filling that was manufactured in Taiwan and is full of extra sugar and sodium and actually isn't made from pumpkins at all, but buttercup squash, which you can also buy from the farmer's market, and even if you don't eat it immediately you can leave it on a shelf in your pantry (if you have one) at room temperature for two years before it spoils. And even if it spoils you can throw it on the compost heap and next summer you will have enough squash to fill up the entire flatbed of a Ford F-150 pick-up truck.

The farmers don't hire snappy young students in neat uniforms and nifty little hats to sell their stuff. They do it themselves, after waking at four AM to harvest it. The older ones, way past retirement age, hobble about on worn-out knees and struggle to count out your change with ham-sized hands whose fingers are warped out of shape from sixty years of back-breaking physical labour. They greet you with a warm, toothless smile and their leathered faces are brutal testimony to the multiple decades of exposure to the sun, wind, rain and frost that even the most battle-scarred soldier would be reluctant to endure.

So, I went back to the grocery store to figure out how much money I would have spent if I had bought my vegetables there, rather than directly from the farmers. It was a bit complicated, because at the grocery store, most items are sold by weight or volume, whereas at the market they are sold by unit, regardless of size or quantity. I had to weigh my tomatoes and squash and zucchini and bell peppers to see how much I had paid per pound or kilo, then compare with the grocery store prices.

For example, you can buy a fist-sized (imported) broccoli at the grocery store for $2.50, or another one (locally grown and hand-picked that very morning) the size of your head at the market for one dollar. That's probably a ten-for-one price difference.

When I was uncertain, I deliberately erred in favour of the grocery store, and not only did I compare apples to apples, but specifically Cortlands to Cortlands and MacIntoshes to MacIntoshes, so to speak.

The result was ugly but predictable. Item for item, across the board from aubergines to green beans, an $80 purchase at the market including fourteen varieties of products translated to a $240 purchase at the grocery store for exactly the same products, on the same day, even though most of the produce at the grocery store was proudly labelled "weekly special" and "local produce."

I didn't bother costing the "bio" produce, because it's the exactly the same stuff but twice the price. You pay for the container, not the content. And either way, the wrapping is not recyclable.

So, what's the difference?

Most farmers don't have Olympic-sized heated swimming pools in their barns, nor do they have to leave their Ferraris out in the rain because their ten-car garage is already full of Porsches and Audis and vintage convertible Corvettes and Mustang Shelbys. That horrible burden belongs to the grocers, who used to earn as much as the barber or the baker or the candle-stick maker, but now have to scramble to find overseas tax havens to hide their multiple millions from the government.

The irony here is that there were more people at the grocery store than at the market, even though they are ten minutes apart by car, bus or bike.

There are people who actually believe that a vegetable with a bit of soil on it will absolutely kill you even after you've washed it, and that if it isn't sanitized and wrapped in plastic, or if it has a spot on it or is even slightly overripe, it is fatally toxic. And the kids who work at the grocery store actually believe that cauliflower and brussels sprouts and eggs and honey are manufactured in a factory in India from recycled t-shirts and old running shoes.

Some people want exactly forty-five tomatoes, no more, no less, and they will pay more for the privilege. Others want exactly six bulbs of garlic, rather than eight, and they will also gladly pay more. Most people are happy to spend three times as much on groceries than they need to. That's 300% more. If you're buying "bio," that's six times more (600%) for exactly the same thing.

These are the same people that absolutely freak out when their municipal taxes or electricity or internet bill increases by less than 2%, but will gladly spend $1,000 for a telephone, plus $400 per month or more for services and apps. My mortgage doesn't cost that much.

And yes, some people require waterproof telephones because they take them into the shower. They actually shampoo with one hand and text and tweet and surf and like and subscribe with the other. As my mom used to say, multitasking is the most efficient way to fuck up every chore as fast as possible.

Maybe people should eat more locally-grown vegetables. Maybe then they might just be a little bit less constipated.

SLIPPERS

I LIKE SLIPPERS.

Once upon a time I had a really comfortable pair of slippers, the kind that we used to call Mules.

A thick sole with an open heel, and a great big dome of felt over the toes. The kind of slippers that you could practically live in for an entire weekend. You slip 'em on Saturday morning, with or without socks, and slide your feet out reluctantly on Sunday evening, when you prepare for the workie morrow.

So, one Saturday morning I woke up earlier than usual, but it was autumn so all was dark, in and out, but something was amiss. The dog barked, and chickens, normally still somnambulant, could be heard arguing. I slipped on my slippers and slipped out the door.

As it turned out it was a false alarm, but I realized sometime later that my nocturnal excursion had caused me to step in poo. Whether it was a fresh gift from my beloved Australian Shepherd dog, Masha, or remnants from my free-range chickens who regularly regale me around my front door was quite moot. Shit is shit.

I like to warn visitors that the property is built on an ancient native burial ground that is haunted by the ghost of the venerable chief *Stepinpoo*.

The soles of my wonderful slippers were thickly buttered with pungent excrement, to which had adhered an abundance of extraneous vegetable and mineral matter, notably straw and twigs and leaves and gravel and feathers.

A little patience would have allowed me to grow prize-winning tomatoes from the soles of those slippers, but that morning I chose to leave them on the doorstep and return to the comfort of my blankets.

Later that day I decided to redeem my precious footwear. I brought them to a bucket of fresh rain-water, and duly scrubbed the soles with a foot-brush until all trace of the accident had disappeared. I then diligently attached them to the clothes-line and allowed the autumn sun and wind to finish the job, and then attended to other matters.

As life is so short, and as you all have noticed that as we go from this to that, certain small chores tend to be neglected, you may have already guessed that the slippers were forgotten that evening, and the next morning I discovered them blown onto the lawn, totally saturated by a brief but torrential rainfall during the night.

I picked them up and lovingly placed them on a small service table in the garden, where I knew that they would enjoy the full benefit of an entire afternoon in the sun. Bees and flies happily buzzed over them, but such well-laid plans are soon laid to rest, and our best intentions are often foiled.

The evening turned sour and drizzly, the slippers remained on the table, and overnight the frost came down hard.

The next morning my poor slippers were frozen solid, like two small bricks. Had I lashed them to a wooden handle, I could have used them to chop firewood.

"Don't worry," my wife said. "I'll take care of your slippers."

So, she lit a fire in the wood stove in the basement, and parked the slippers on top. Before long, they began to steam and melt, and it seemed as if all was right in the world.

Until the soles of the slippers began to produce a toxic smoke that set off the fire alarm. The dog began to hurl. We leapt to the stove to remove the slippers, but they had stuck from the heat. I grabbed the little shovel that we use to remove the ashes, and scraped the smoking footwear off of the surface of the stove, and ran outside to dump them in a bucket of water.

My wife followed me out, then removed the slippers from the bucket of water, shook them like a dog stepping out of the lake, and hung them by the heels on the clothes line.

"It's gonna be ten below tonight," she said. "But tomorrow morning the sun will rise again. Your slippers will be fine as new!"

MILKWEED

I LIKE MILKWEED.

When I was a kid, there were literally clouds of monarch butterflies. And there were fields of milkweed. It grew absolutely everywhere. We loved the seed pods, and we had numerous names for them. Cocottes, moutons. We would split the unripe pods in our hands and admire the soft, silky, bright white fibres within, and diligently wipe our tiny fists on our clothes as the milky white sap oozed onto our skin. And in August, when the pods spontaneously burst and spread their seeds, we would grab fistfuls of dry stalks and spin them in the air and watch as thousands of tiny silver parachutes would catch the breeze and flit about us like wild things.

Nobody told us back then that the monarch butterflies depended on those plants to survive. Nobody ever made the link.

Ten years ago, I stopped mowing my lawn. It was a sequence of events that led me to that.

My mom, before she died, had paid for me a subscription to a Canadian ecological magazine whose name I forget. There was one article that I enjoyed in particular, in which the author claimed that if each and every one of us left a tiny part of our own property unattended, then it would create a patchwork network of wilderness that would enable our wildlife, if not to prosper, at least to endure.

So, I stopped mowing my lawn. And HOO BOY nature doesn't take its time! Now every year I've got a chest-high meadow of tall weeds that I can barely wade through. Queen Anne's Lace, Goldenrod, Virginia Creeper, Dandelion, Wild Pea, Plantain, Clover, Lamb's Quarters, Wild Sumac, Thistles, black raspberries, red raspberries, wild blackberries, ferns, chicory, mint, thyme, and oregano and dozens of other native species that I haven't even identified yet.

I expected a backlash from my neighbours, some of whom spend thousands of dollars a year on maintaining a golf-green, weed-free lawn. I even expected to have to go to court over my right to grow weeds, so I decided to prepare my arguments in advance.

I went back to the magazine that my mom had bought me, and re-read the article about leaving a bit of space for "native species." So, I called my weeds "native species." Then I flipped to the letterhead, and I noticed that one of the editors was none other than Michaele Jean, the Governor General of Canada at the time, who was the representative of the Queen of England, her Majesty Queen Elizabeth II, by the grace of God. That monarch, by the way, was the supreme leader of Canada, in case you didn't know.

So now I had my argument. The magazine endorses the cultivation of native species. The magazine is endorsed by the Governor General, who speaks for the Queen of England, who was chosen by God. And If you don't believe that last fact, just pull any coin out of your pocket. It clearly states, Elisabeth II D. G. Regina, that is, Dei Gratia (by the grace of God, Queen).

So, if the Queen wants it, then God wants it too, since He specifically chose her to long reign over us, happy and glorious, sent here victorious. I rest my case. The weeds stay, by the grace of God. Actually, that's a given; any moron with an ounce of sense can figure that one out without having to remove their shoes and socks in order to count their toes.

Fortunately, I never had to litigate the thing. Others have been less fortunate.

In certain communities, weeds on the lawn are considered a crime, and the perpetrators are duly prosecuted.

But I had a shortage of milkweed on my property, and I wanted more. So, one day I went to the local *dépanneur* (in Quebec that's a corner shop or convenience store), and I noticed that there was a truckload of milkweed growing in their flower box, which incidentally was entirely populated with native species (i.e., weeds).

I love going to the local dépanneur. It is owned by a Chinese family that exclusively speaks Mandarin. The only French that you ever get out of them is a rote-learned phrase "messy buzzoo" (*merci bonjour*, or thank you, good day) or "messy buzzoonay" (*merci bonne journée*, or, thank you, good day). Their English is even worse. They haven't quite figured out yet that they are no longer living in Manchuria. But their weed garden in front of the store is magnificent.

So, I decided to benefit from their expertise. They had milkweed to beat the band, and in every stage of development.

I stepped out of the store, and removed all of the items from the plastic bag that they had given me, and proceeded to harvest the ripe heads of milkweed that were already spilling their seeds onto the parking lot and across the street. I avoided the seed pods that were not yet open, as well as those that were already spreading their joy, and gathered up only those that were in between. I stuffed my bounty into the plastic bag, but I did not close it because the residual moisture would have caused my harvest to rot.

I then tossed the bag into the back seat of my car and forgot all about it.

For those who don't know me, my Honda Civic is a trundling experiment in what not to do with a car. Only the most intrepid or desperate hitchhiker will cast aside the rotting pumpkins and bags of soil and cement and coils of filthy garden hose and discarded garments, small stones and vintage hardware and a host of other unidentifiable dross in the front seat for the privilege of riding shotgun for a few miles, and only God knows what's in the trunk. It might be road kill, but from what year? Dead animals don't come with millesime labels.

So that big bag stuffed full of milkweed seeds sat on the back seat for several weeks, amongst the waste lumber and old newspapers and cardboard boxes and soda cans and other trash, and one day a few dried seeds decided to make their escape.

If you have ever seen a milkweed seed, you will agree with me that it is like watching a tiny fragile angel fly. They are like dandelions, only bigger and whiter and fluffier and with way more personality.

So initially a few of the seeds began to flit about the cabin of the car, carried by the random eddies generated by the heater fan and the slightly open window, and before long I had a mini-snowstorm swirling around me.

Some of the parachutes stopped to rest on the dashboard, where they clustered together like a family church choir and continued to bobble up and down in harmony, animating my commute. Others swirled around my head, and facetiously landed on my nose and eyelashes like Julie Andrews' favourite snowflakes, and some were sucked outside of the car through the slash in the slightly lowered window, and I felt like Johnny Appleseed, randomly spreading this wonderful joy across the landscape as I drove by, and each seed seemed to have a will of its own, to stay and dashboard dance, or to depart and take its chances.

A few months ago, there was a seminar in Montreal on how to make our world green again. Everybody who attended received a tiny pot with a meadow flower growing in it. I hope that some of the participants got milkweed, and that they were able to plant it in a place where it could prosper.

PS. The bag is still in my car, somewhere …

MASTURBATION

I LIKE MASTURBATION.

OK. Please try and convince me that you have never ever twiddled your twat or beat your meat. Even children do it. It's the most sensitive and the most manually accessible part of your body. It's as if God purposefully designed us all to auto-eroticize from birth. You don't need somebody else to do it for you; you can handle it all by yourself.

Of course, if somebody else can do it for you, that's OK too, but typically we call that foreplay, which is usually a preamble to actual sex, but not all the time.

I'm talking about you, all by yourself.

Some people say that easy access to internet porn has erased our inner fantasies and made unassisted masturbation difficult or impossible. I beg to differ. Whereas porn makes masturbation quicker and easier, I truly love to linger on youthful exploits in the moments before I fall asleep.

And, oddly, the most successful of my fantasies are not with the girls that I actually had sex with, but rather the ones that got away, so to speak. The seduction failures, the missed opportunities. The flat-out rejections, the face-slappers. I will leave it to brighter minds than mine to figure that one out, psychologically.

My favourite cartoonists in the 1980s were Reiser and Wolinski, who both drew for the iconic French magazine *Harakiri*, which eventually morphed into *Charlie Hebdo*.

Reiser died quite young, but left behind his legacy. His main character, a fat, unshaved, unwashed, grotesque character by the name of "*Gros Dégueulasse*" (literally, fat, disgusting person) would promenade about Paris in nothing but his oversized soiled underpants and wreak havoc while spouting philosophical truisms. The entire episodes were drawn in a childish scrawl that emphasized the iconoclastic nature of the main character.

Gros Dégueulasse would justify his urine-soaked underwear by claiming that the yellow stains were, in fact, gold plating.

Reiser's best friend and collaborator was Georges Wolinski.

Wolinski is well known for several characters, including Gaston La Bite, who had a forty-foot-long penis, which caused him considerable embarrassment in social gatherings. (Gaston, not Georges.)

Another one of his iconic characters was Cactus Joe, who, as a new-born baby, was abandoned by his mother in the deserts just north of St-Tropez. The cactus raised him as one of their own, so he grew up covered with prickly spines, and when he reached puberty he would ogle the pretty, bikini-clad girls on the beach with lust in his eyes, knowing that he could never ever go there or do that. This is Kafka-esque alienation wrapped in a funny cartoon.

These men were true iconoclasts, trashing the barriers and stereotypes that our society so willingly clings to.

On January 7th, 2015, the Islamists had had just about enough of this nonsense. They burst into the editorial offices of *Charlie Hebdo* in Paris and mowed down all ten cartoonists with machine guns. Cartoonists. That was their specific target. People who draw funny pictures that make people laugh. Wolinski was among them.

Some people have absolutely no sense of humour.

Actually, they were specifically irked about the cartoonists' depictions of their sacred leader, Mahomet. He didn't need to masturbate; he married ten-year-old girls instead, and they would have gladly done that for him, and whatever else he required from them.

Getting back to the subject, one of my favourite Wolinski cartoons is when the young Wolinski (18-ish) surprises the old Wolinski (forty-ish) in the bathroom with a girlie magazine in one hand and his erect penis firmly in the other. (That's the same Wolinski, old and young, and not father and son.)

The young Wolinski is astonished. "I thought that, by your age, you didn't have to jerk off anymore!" To which the older, wiser Wolinski replies, "Nuance, my son! We, the older generation, we masturbate for sheer pleasure, whereas you, the youth, must do so from absolute necessity."

So, go ahead. Beat your meat; twiddle your twat. Haul out a tub of lard and grease it up. Think about all the nasty dirty secret sexy things that you did, or didn't do but always wanted to. Dwell on missed opportunities. Pile up some pillows under your butt, pull up your knees, spread your thighs and poke a polite greasy fingertip incrementally up your previously puritan tight little virgin asshole.

Nobody is going to come around and blow you to smithereens with a machine gun for that.

At least, not yet. I hope not.

HOLES

I LIKE HOLES.

Addendum to Ecclesiastes.

While digging a decent grave for my recently departed and dearly beloved cat Ti-Nou, I wondered if the great and wise King Solomon had not skipped a line or two.

A time to dig a hole, a time to fill one up.

Or maybe my reflections are redundant, like a hole in my mind that needs to be filled with more wisdom-fill than uncle Solomon can shovel in. Maybe my fond memories of that stupid cat will be enough to fill the hole between my ears.

Is a hole a thing unto itself, or merely the absence of stuff?

Digging a hole is a strange experience. You obviously don't dig a hole just because you're bored. It has to fulfill some useful purpose. But the act of doing it seems so abjectly futile.

Whether you're planting a potato or burying a cat or digging a well, you know that you're gonna fill up that hole when you're done, so it all seems a bit futile.

Archeologists dig holes in order to dig up holes that people dug hundreds or thousands of years ago. They find in their holes all kinds of other holes, all of which were filled in with shit after the people dug them.

Post-holes that held up Saxon mansions. Latrine holes that contain coprolites, or fossilized shit, reveal what Vikings ate.

Garbage pits that tell us what medieval mansions were made of. Caves where our ancestors painted during the Ice Age. Deep wells that allow people to live in desert climates, and tiny cracks in the Wailing Wall into which worshipers can slide a tiny prayer hand-scrabbled onto a scrap of paper. Foxholes that soldiers dig to prevent their heads from being blown off while they sleep in the cold mud, only to have their faces blown off the minute that they step out of them. Black holes in the universe where the rules of nature break down forever. The cold black underground hole that you and I will spend eternity in. The warm, soft, moist, dark vagina that we all emerged from.

We dig huge holes in order to extract substances that make us wealthy, then self-flagellate because those same horrible holes are somehow impoverishing us, then dig even bigger holes to safely store the precious metals that we so eagerly extracted. Holes that provide us with fossil fuels are really ugly. Holes that provide us with lithium and rare earths in order to build batteries for electric machines are pretty ugly too. And the holes that we will have to dig to bury all of the discarded plastic and batteries we make will have to be far bigger than the vast holes left in our collective souls.

Some holes are extremely useful. But they can also injure or kill you. So please, show a bit of respect for holes.

All of this reminds me of one particular hole.

My dad emigrated from Switzerland after WW2, and coming from a country where land is measured in square centimeters, when he got to Canada he naturally wanted to buy as much land as he could afford, which wasn't really a whole lot. Actually, it was an entire lot; just not a big one. He then decided to use it to erect a giant monument to human stupidity, and thirty years later it killed him. That was in 1982.

The reason that it took him thirty years to raise his monument is that he refused to use electric tools. That was cheating. This is Canada after all, where for centuries intrepid pioneers cut down entire forests with their teeth and built huge cities with one bare hand while fighting off native savages and wild bears with the other.

The reason that he thought that it would take no time at all is that he actually had an apprentice to do the heavy lifting.

That was me, and as of the age of about seven or eight I was enlisted to haul the water, mix the cement, split the stones, saw the wood and sift the sand, and if I cried he wouldn't hesitate to knock out one of my teeth in order to teach me what is was like to be a real man.

Today people like that go to prison, or to the psych ward, but back then it was just considered normal behaviour.

So, he built his country house, and it was almost all bad. He claimed that there were only three ways to do a job. Your way, my way, and the right way. He did it all his way, like Frank Sinatra. That is to say, the fourth, or wrong way.

Ten years after he died, my mom still had me up there every weekend fixing shit that he got wrong or finishing shit that he never got around to doing.

This one particular weekend was a bit different. It was July, the best part of the year, when most of the civilized world is on vacation. Not me. I had to fix something, repair something, or build something. Family traditions do not die easily, no matter how ill-conceived they may be.

Unfortunately, there was nothing left to fix that month. No more leaky pipes, no bad electrical circuits, no leaking roof tiles, no firewood to chop and stack.

That put my mom in a serious snit. The idea of me just sitting around, enjoying the sun for once in my life was more than she could endure. I could see it coming.

Breakfast on Saturday morning.

"We've got moles," she said, pouting, as if the damn things had just declared war on us.

So what? The darned critters were there way before we came along, and will probably endure long after we depart. They'll probably nibble our toes when we go six feet under.

"You have to get rid of them."

Okey-dokey, I'll get right on it. Off to the hardware store.

The clerk had some wonderful products to allow me to fulfill my task. Abundant amounts of rat poison, or a wonderful little bomb that I can use to blow them up. I just insert it in the hole, light the fuse, and presto! No more moles.

Anything else? Nope, but a decent dose of both will solve your problem overnight!

"So, I can poison them, or blow them up?"

"Or both!"

OK. Thank you. Lemme sleep on it.

Back at the ranch, my eager mom wants to know what I bought.

"They got nothing for moles, mom," I said, lying.

Crestfallen, she implores me to intervene. Her very life seems to depend on the outcome.

"Lemme think about it." And I did. I sat on the kitchen steps in the blistering sun thinking about how to extract the moles from under the ground.

If I had a mole magnet, then all I had to do was dangle it over the ground and the little beasts would come popping out of their hidey-holes, pop-pop-pop, and the problem would be solved. But I only had one afternoon, and inventing a mole magnet would probably take a bit longer than that.

I needed another strategy.

So, what do moles do, anyways? They eat and sleep and poop and fornicate just like everybody else, including me. Maybe not all at once or in any particular order, but still …

Moles dig holes. Shit, I can do that. I need a shovel.

So, I haul out the garden spade and start to dig, right in front of the kitchen door. Because if there are any moles to be got, kitchen door moles are probably the best ones to get. Don't ask me why; it's some kind of rule.

I don't know how deep to dig, but I figure if I was a mole I'd like to live just under the grass roots in summer, but at least three feet down under the frost line in winter, so four feet down seems just about right. After an hour or so I have delved a tidy trench, six feet in diameter and four feet deep.

By now the summer sun is high in the sky, I'm sweating like a horse, and the soil around the inside of my pit is drying out and crumbling away to the bottom. I still haven't seen a single mole, but, to hopelessly misquote Alanis Morissette, I'm tired but I'm healthy; I'm lost but I'm hopeful. I'm sitting there on the kitchen steps, admiring my handiwork, watching the little clumps of soil tumble down into the pit as they dry in the hot sun, when suddenly I spot something unusual.

A little bit of dirt seems to be jumping away from the canyon wall, rather than just crumbling down, and it is followed by a tiny little whiskered nose smaller than a pebble. The curious mole has come to the excavation site to find out what is going on. I rise slowly, carefully, silently, and pick up the shovel. I walk stealthily to the site and then, with a single blow, I stab the steel blade into the ground about six inches behind the white whiskers.

The mole, panicked by the shock, turns back into its tunnel only to run nose-first into a solid steel wall. Now frenzied with fear, it turns around again and bursts suicidally headlong into the pit, where it scurries about helplessly at the bottom in search of refuge. All I have to do now is bend over and pick it up.

Now I am confronted with another problem. The last thing that I had expected from this whole exercise was to actually catch a mole. The whole song-and-dance was just a charlatan charade to show my mom that I was willing to waste an entire day on useless, backbreaking chores that served absolutely no useful purpose whatsoever, as usual, in return for which she would cook me a hearty meal and call me a good boy, as usual. That was the routine, and it was more for her benefit than my own. I was more than capable of buying, cooking and eating my own food, but from her perspective that was a pathological behaviour, a total rejection of her maternal love for her son.

And now I'm stuck with a fucking live mole cowering in my fist.

So, I walked to the garden shed and found a five-gallon plastic bucket and parked the critter in the bottom and watched it scamper around in circles like the frightened little furry blind rodent that it was. I then carried the bucket back to the excavation site and threw a few spadefuls of damp earth into the container so that the prisoner would feel a bit less exposed. I then sat down on the step in the hot sun and waited to see if the experiment could be repeated.

My mom came out and asked me why I was just sitting there doing absolutely nothing useful. I told her that I was resting and could I please have a glass of water. I didn't show her the bucket.

An hour later I had five of the little buggers. It was probably only a tiny fraction of the total population, but it was enough for a day's work. I brought the bucket into the kitchen and sat down at the table. My mom asked me why I wasn't outside working. So, I plucked one of the little beasts out of the soil, and held it up to her. The tiny aubergine-colored ball of fur had a belly white as snow, which is astonishing for an animal that spends its life burrowing in filth. It was totally defenseless in my hand and in a very obvious state of distress.

"There's your moles. What should I do with them? I can bash them with a rock, or just tie them in a bag and toss them in the lake. You decide."

She actually bent over to observe the other specimens scurrying about in the loose dirt at the bottom of the bucket.

"That's OK," she said. "You can let them go."

And so I did. Then I came back in the house.

"Supper's in an hour. I'm making pork chops."

"No thanks, mom. I think I've got sunstroke. I'm just gonna go to bed."

"You didn't fill up the hole!"

"Tomorrow, mom. I'll fill up the hole tomorrow. I promise."

So yeah. A little respect for holes. Even crusty old ladies with good intentions and bad ideas can take a life lesson from at least one of them. And moles seem to like some kind of holes (particularly the ones that they dig all by themselves) and dislike others, like the one I dug, and it would be difficult to muster up a credible argument to refute that.

THERMODYNAMICS FOR KIDS

I LIKE THERMODYNAMICS.

So, what the heck is electricity anyways?

Basically, electricity is electrons moving through a conductor.

Seems simple. But the conductor is not an orchestra leader or a bus driver, and electrons are, well ... funny little things, to say the least. In order to understand, we have to start from the beginning ...

To a physicist, there are only two kinds of stuff in the universe; matter and energy. As it turns out, they are both aspects of the same thing, but that's not our problem right now.

The matter-half of the universe, that is to say, the hard, heavy stuff like rocks and trees and chairs, and even some softer stuff like water, air and feathers, is all made up of matter, and matter is made up of atoms.

Individual atoms are among the smallest objects in the universe; so small that nobody can actually see them, even with the most sophisticated equipment. But they tend to lump up together in very large quantities to form the various types of things that make up the physical universe, like chairs and trees and mountains and stars.

So, what are atoms made of?

Since we can't actually see them, nobody can say for sure what exactly is inside an atom, and scientists are still arguing about this today. Nonetheless, by doing various experiments like banging them together at very high speeds, we can see how they react with each other and then we can make a pretty good guess as to what falls out after the impact, kind of like crashing two cars together and then looking at the various parts that are left over after the accident to see what the smashed cars had inside.

One hundred years ago, scientists believed that an atom was a tiny, hard ball that held a positive electric charge, surrounded by a cloud of even tinier hard balls that each held a negative charge. While this description is not a completely accurate one, it suits us fine as far as explaining electricity is concerned.

The big part in the middle of the atom is called the nucleus, and it is itself made up of even smaller parts, of which there are two different kinds. One kind holds the positive electrical charge and is therefore named the proton. The other kind is very nearly the same size as the proton, but has no electrical charge whatsoever. Since it is electrically neutral, it is called a neutron. Only the proton, with its positive electrical charge, is important in electricity. The neutron, being by definition neutral, does not play a role in electric events, and so we will not be talking about it much today.

The tiny particles that fly around the nucleus have a net negative charge, and they are called electrons. Now picture a bag of positively charged billiard balls with a bunch of negatively charged mosquitoes buzzing around it, and you have a working model of an atom. It is by no means an accurate model, but it explains electricity very well so we will use it. Why these particles have these very specific properties no one can say; that's just the way they are.

There are exactly 103 different types of atoms; these make up absolutely every piece of matter in the universe. Each type of atom has a name so we can tell them apart, and every group of identical atoms is called an element. If you want to learn their names you can look up the Periodic Table of the Elements in a dictionary or on the internet. The difference in the different types of atoms is how many protons they contain. So, the smallest atom on the list is called Hydrogen, which has only one proton, so the nucleus has a net positive charge of +1. The next one up the list is named Helium, with 2 protons, and so on, one proton at a time, all the way up to 103. In theory, the numbers could go up and up and up forever, way past 103 to 500 or 5000 or more. In reality, these big bundles of particles are quite unstable. Like a house of cards, it starts out OK, but the higher up you go the shakier it gets until the whole thing comes tumbling down in a heap. So far, 103 is as high as the universe has been able to go before the atomic house of cards all falls down, and even the last twenty or so are hobbling about on very wobbly knees.

Now imagine that the positive nucleus is your head, and the electron-mosquitoes are buzzing around you. As long as the mosquitoes are near your head, the entire combination of head plus mosquitoes has a net electrical charge of zero, since the positive charge on your head and the negative charge on the mosquitoes cancel each other out. If you swoosh the bugs away, or if they smell something better somewhere else, like your baby sister or your mom or a big fat smelly cow, they might fly away and leave you alone. This is exactly what happens to atoms sometimes; the electrons smell something better somewhere else, and they fly off, leaving the poor nucleus with a net positive charge. Wherever the electron-bugs flew off to will have a surplus of negatively-charged electron-bugs, and so that place will have an overall negative charge. But this is only a temporary situation; the natural attraction between the negative and positive particles means that eventually the electrons will fly back to wherever they came from, like your head. (The electrons move about more freely than the much larger and heavier protons.) If you've ever been camping in the woods, you'll know exactly what I'm talking about.

This separating and returning of particles happens naturally every day, like when you shuffle around on the carpet in your stocking feet, then touch the metal doorknob. The shuffling attracts lots of electrons which cling to your clothes, giving you a net negative charge and leaving the electron-deprived carpet with an overall positive charge. Naturally, when you touch a metal object the electrons all go rushing back out at the same time, in order to return to the carpet. This creates a spark, and even though you can't see or touch an individual electron, the spark looks and feels very real indeed! (Sometimes you can even smell the electrons! The energy released by the spark can cause a chemical reaction in the air. Oxygen in the atmosphere, which we breathe all the time but is completely odourless, is converted into ozone, which has a funny 'electric' smell.)

This simple experiment shows us two things. First of all, we can twiddle the electrons to force them to move around, and second, when we do so we can create a source of energy.

Unfortunately, our carpet-rubbing game is not very helpful, since we didn't create a whole lot of energy, and the little bit that we did make is rather difficult to control. What we need is to find a way to safely store up large quantities of electrons, then release them in a regular, predictable manner.

But before we get to that, we need to understand a little bit about the second big thing that the universe contains, that is to say, energy.

When I said that our carpet experience created energy, I wasn't completely truthful. The fact is, neither energy nor matter can be created nor destroyed. All of the energy and all of the matter in the universe was there to begin with, and the same amount of energy and matter will always exist now and forever, amen. They can, however, be transformed from one type to another. In the case of matter, atoms can combine with each other to create different substances. A nice shiny new nail in a puddle of water will eventually turn into a hunk of rust. In this case, oxygen atoms dissolved in the water are combining with iron atoms in the nail to create iron oxide, which is the chemical name for rust. If you added up the weight of the nail and the weight of the oxygen before the process began, it would be exactly equal to the weight of the rust at the end, no more, no less. This is so always exactly true in every transformation that it is considered a natural law, and is called the Law of Conservation of Mass.

So, what about energy? It so happens that energy also exists in different forms, all of which can be converted from one type to another under the right conditions. Like matter, these energy transformations result in just as much energy as was put in at the beginning. Also, like matter, energy is neither created nor destroyed, and this principle is called the Law of Conservation of Energy. (As a footnote, it is also possible to convert energy into mass and vice versa. These are called nuclear reactions because the atom's nucleus is very much involved.) Heat and light from the sun, as well as electricity from nuclear power plants, are produced in this way. That said, the total sum of all the energy and all the mass is always the exactly the same before and after, and this is called the Law of Conservation of … you guessed it! … Mass and Energy!)

Let's look at some different types of energy. Keep in mind that all of the energy in the universe was already there to begin with; all we can do is fiddle with it and change it from one type to another, like Lego blocks. The box only contains a finite (limited) number of pieces, but they can be put together and taken apart again to create a very large variety of things.

One very common type of energy is called kinetic energy. The name comes from a Latin word which means 'movement,' so kinetic energy is the energy of moving things. (Another word with the same root is 'cinema,' a French word which is an abbreviation of a bigger word that literally translates as 'moving pictures,' which the Americans eventually shortened to 'movies,' and you know that everybody loves a good movie!)

The most obvious source of kinetic energy is … you and me! We're always moving about, and even when we're sitting or lying down we are still moving our fingers and toes, blinking our eyes, and so on. Even if you're fast asleep, your lungs and heart are still moving, collecting oxygen and pumping it through your body to keep you alive, even while you sleep.

Other things that move, like wind and cars and basketballs, are also creating kinetic energy. But we just said that energy cannot be created …

So where does the energy come from that allows us and cars and basketballs to move around? Cars and people create kinetic energy by changing another type of energy into movement. The energy source that we use is called chemical energy, because it is stored in chemical substances, like sugar and gasoline.

Now, I wouldn't want to drink gasoline or put sugar in my gas tank, but the chemical reactions that make us and our cars move are very much the same. Chemically speaking, both gas and sugar are very similar. (They contain the same types of atoms.) When these substances combine with oxygen, we say that they oxidize or burn. This releases the chemical energy that is stored up inside, which can then be converted into movement. The difference between the car and you is that the car burns its fuel very fast, otherwise it would just trundle along at a snail's pace, which isn't much help, whereas we burn our fuel much more slowly, which is also good because if we converted our fuel as fast as cars do, we would explode like hand grenades.

So where did the energy come from that was stored in the sugar and the gas? In both cases, it came from … the Sun!

We can feel the Sun's heat and see its light, and many other types of energy come from the sun which are invisible to us but can be detected using special instruments. Radio waves from the

Sun can be 'heard' using big antennas. Our big flaming ball in the sky also sends us microwaves, just like the ones we use in our kitchens, as well as ultraviolet waves, which burn our skin on a hot summer day.

All of these are forms of energy, but the one that concerns us here is visible light. Green plants use their leaves like antennas, soaking up the light from the Sun. They then take atoms (!) from the air around them and the water in the ground, and use the solar energy to build new chemicals, just like the box of Lego blocks. Sugar is only one kind of thing that plants can make; there are very many more. When we eat the parts of the plant that have stored the Sun's energy in chemicals, our body does the exact opposite of what the plant did. It breaks up the Lego blocks and releases the stored energy. Fortunately, it converts it to kinetic energy, rather than back into light, otherwise we would stay perfectly still and glow like neon signs! The Lego-block atoms go back into the box, that is, the water and the air, to be used again later by other plants.

Cars do the exact same thing, except that the plants that did the job of storing the energy in the gasoline actually lived a very long time ago. Millions of years ago, to be a bit more precise, without really being very much more precise at all. Various plants soaked up the sun's energy and stored it away in chemicals (combinations of atoms), just like plants do today.

Gasoline comes from petroleum, which is another Latin word, and it means oil from rocks, or oily rocks, or rocky oil, which either way is a pretty good description. Petroleum is basically oil, and it is found under the ground (in rocks, or rather, squished between layers of rocks like a giant subterranean rock-oil lasagna). It is basically left over from shellfish, like clams or oysters, that ate tiny plants in the ocean, who in turn were busy storing the Sun's energy the same way that plants do today. As the shellfish died, they piled up at the bottom of the sea and were covered by sand. Then more shells, more sand, and so on for a very, very long time.

Eventually the sand and shells got compressed into rocks and the animals got squished into petroleum, from which we make gas for our cars. It is no coincidence that one of the biggest producers of gasoline in the world is called Shell, and that its corporate logo is … a sea shell! Another big name, Sunoco, is an abbreviation of Sun Oil Corporation, which tells you where the energy came from before it ended up in the seashell!

Actually, all of what I just told you is a big lie. When I was in grade school, my teachers told me that petroleum came from shellfish living in the ocean millions of years ago, but they lied to me, and I innocently repeated that lie to you. My bad.

Actually, petroleum is made up from tiny slimy critters called algae. Yes, the same stinky green stuff that fouls up your swimming pool and poisons your fish aquarium. That is what petroleum is made of.

As for the sea shells, they got deposited elsewhere and became calcite, which is a kind of rock.

So, what do the Egyptian pyramids of Giza, the Supreme Court Building in Washington, DC, the Greek Acropolis, Saint Paul's cathedral in London and the White Cliffs of Dover all have in common? They are all made from different forms of calcite (limestone, chalk and marble) which is the leftover shells from all of the sea critters. It's the mushy stuff between the shells that ended up as petroleum.

So now what did the Sun do to produce so much light? As I mentioned before, the Sun produces energy by converting matter in a process (nuclear energy) which is far more complicated than I can explain here and not really necessary to understand our main subject, which is (or was supposed to be) electricity.

Speaking of which, what is electrical energy anyways? Good question.

But before we can answer, we need a word from our sponsors. No, sorry; I meant to say that we need to understand one more form of energy. I am talking about heat energy, of course.

Heat energy is the black sheep of the energy family, the odd man out, the bottom-of-the-barrel left-over outcast of the energy clan. Surely, heat is useful. We need it to cook our food and keep us from freezing our butts! But from a scientific point of view, heat is a straggler, a hanger-on, a parasitic welfare-bum spare-change street-corner busking hustler in the house of energy conversion. In the royal energy hierarchy, heat is low man on the totem pole, first on the compost heap. Heat is energetic garbage, the last lump of unusable stuff after all of the cream has been lapped up. Heat is the devil, the serpent in the Garden, and at the end of time, heat and heat alone will be guilty of the murder and ultimate death of the universe.

Okay, that may seem a little bit harsh and overly dramatic, and on the up side, the so-called 'heat-death' of the universe, as scientists call it, is not actually scheduled until several billion years from now, so we can relax a bit longer. Nevertheless, heat is a big problem. So much so, in fact, that there is a field of science that does nothing but watch heat move around, much like a detective watches criminal suspects move around in the hopes of catching them red-handed or finding evidence against them so that he can put them behind bars and prevent them from doing more harm, or at least restrict their movements so that they can't act as freely as they would want to.

The study of heat moving around is called thermodynamics. This is also from Latin, and it translates as such: thermo = heat, and dynamics = moving around. Hence the name. (Who said Latin is complicated?) OK. I know you're going to call me in on this one. I have proof. The opposite of 'dynamic' is 'static,' which means, 'not moving around.' So there!

The problem is that heat is a thief, a criminal mastermind. Every single time that we try to use energy for other needs, heat comes along and steals some of our energy and wastes it. When you run and play, you get hot. That's really annoying, and to boot you get tired because some of the chemical energy that you are using to skate and shoot the puck (kinetic energy) is wasted because it is converted to heat instead, which makes you hot and tired and cranky and thirsty, then you get into a fist fight with another player over nothing at all and the ref benches you and then your dad gets into an argument with the coach and another dad starts yelling at the ref and at your dad and someone calls the cops and you all end up hot and tired and cranky and thirsty in the cop car and at the police station and then you have to explain everything to your mom and you get home really late and the next day you can't do well in school because you're too tired and all your friends know all about the bloody nose you gave the other guy and some of them think it's totally cool but others say you're a total jerk and your teachers are giving you the evil eye because they think you're bad but for the wrong reasons and the girls can't decide if you're totally hot or really a total jerk so they talk about you in whispers behind your back and giggle at you so you can't hear what they're saying about you so you don't know if it's good or bad and the girl you kinda like is giggling with another girl who doesn't really like you at all so is that good or bad we don't know so you just wish that you could turn back time and go back and not get into that fight or that everybody could just shut up for a minute and read your mind and understand that it wasn't your fault or just crawl into a hole and sleep for a hundred years like Rip Van Winkle and when you wake up everyone involved in this will be dead or have forgotten all of this and moved on to bigger and better things. Not very scientific, but that is one of the things that the heat-thief does.

Your parents' car is also a victim of the heat-thief. A few minutes after starting the car, the engine gets very hot. It gets so hot that we have to build in a radiator to pull the heat away from the engine to cool it down; otherwise the engine will get too hot and it will break down. If the car overheats, you're in trouble. If your dad overheats because the car overheats, you're in double-trouble! All the ice cream in the world won't cool that flame.

A large part of the chemical energy from the gasoline that is supposed to move the car forward is being turned into heat energy, rather than kinetic energy (which makes the car move, which is what cars are supposed to do). All of the energy which was converted to heat is totally wasted, and if you've ever gotten close to a car engine after a long drive you know how much heat is coming off that sucker!

Absolutely every single invention of mankind that uses any kind of energy at all is a victim of the heat-thief. Your computer, your television, your light bulbs, they all get hot by turning some of the energy they use into useless heat. Even the refrigerator, which is built to keep things cold on the inside, gets hot on the outside!

Even simple tools like hammers, screwdrivers and wheelbarrows waste some of the energy that we use to make them work. Whack a nail into a piece of wood, then touch the nail's head. It's hot. Screw in a screw, then touch it. It's hot too. (Normally, both the hammer and the screwdriver will have heated up as well, but since they're bigger than the nail or the screw, the heat will be more spread out and more difficult to detect.)

So far, we have seen that different kinds of energy can be changed into other kinds of energy in order to do the job that has to be done, with the heat-thief stealing a part of it every step of the way. Let's briefly go back over our chain of events.

First, the Sun sends us energy in the form of light. Many other forms of energy come from the Sun as well, some of which are harmful to us and others good, but only the part that appears as visible light is used by plants. Plants capture the Sun's energy and change it into chemical energy in the form of sugar or petroleum (and many other kinds as well!) by recombining atoms in the air and water around them into bigger Lego-block units, which we call molecules. After that, we eat the plants' energy-packed molecules and our muscles reverse the process, releasing the stored energy to make us move (kinetic energy). Then, by using that kinetic energy (shuffling our feet over the carpet), we collect electrons on us, which creates electrical energy. When we touch that fateful doorknob, the electrical energy is changed back into visible light energy (the spark that we can see).

There are two main reasons why all of this is important in understanding electricity (which we still haven't talked about!). The first one is because of thermodynamics, which shows us that every time that we change energy from one form to another, we lose a little bit of the useful energy to the heat-thief. That is to say, some of the useful energy is wasted as heat. What this means is that eventually, all of the different kinds of energy in the universe will be completely changed into heat energy, and absolutely nothing else will ever move or change ever again, and the universe will die. Bummer. On the happy side, understanding the heat-thief and how and why he works is essential in understanding how and why electricity works. Electricity only works because the heat-thief makes it work, and if we want to use electricity, we have to play by his rules, for better or for worse.

The other reason is that we use electricity for a very large number of different jobs. We use electricity to create other forms of energy, like the ones we have already looked at. Obviously, sometimes we use it to make heat directly. A stove, a water heater, microwave oven, toaster and electric heater all convert electricity into heat directly.

But we also change electrical energy into light energy. The job of every electric light on the planet is to do precisely that – change electrical energy into visible light energy (the same kind that plants use!) so that we can see what we are doing and where we are going and not have to stumble around in the dark and stub our toes on the furniture. Our TVs and computer screens also convert electricity into visible light energy.

Electrical energy can also be converted to kinetic energy. Any electrical tool or appliance which has moving parts, like a power saw or a kitchen blender or a fan, does exactly that. In fact, this works both ways. Electricity can be used to turn a fan, which makes the air move around. We call moving air wind, and nature produces lots of that (especially after eating a big plate of beans!). But nature's wind can also be used to turn a propeller, which is exactly like a fan, which in turn (no pun intended) can be used to make … electricity!

OK. So now I've managed to bore you to tears with theory, and all that you want to do is sit down, get practical, eat some beans, move some stuff around and build a real, working electrical circuit with real hunks of metal and wire and stuff. You want to light up a light bulb, get a motor turning, operate a rack of switches and relays, witness lights and solenoids. Well, good on you I say, but if you don't get the theory, the reason why everything works, then you'll just end up burning up your light bulbs and motors and fingers and maybe even the whole house. Just like every other kind of real fun, electricity is a bit dangerous. Again, the devil is heat. When the heat-thief invades an uncontrolled electrical circuit, he can start a fire quicker than a match, and in places where you don't expect it. If the doorknob-spark gets bigger than you thought, it can burn your skin and hair right off your bones and send you straight to the emergency room in an ambulance, waiting for a skin graft. (Trust me, you don't want a skin graft. It really, really, really hurts. A lot. An awful lot. How much? More than all of the combined pain that you have ever felt in your entire life, multiplied by infinity, plus a bit more.)

Also, you're a bit too young for a lethal heart attack, but a decent electric shock will definitely give you an idea of what to expect a few years down the road. Electric shocks can fry your brain better than crack cocaine, and leave you paralyzed stupid and brain-dead.

So, are you ready to have some fun?

Well, no. I can hear you screaming from the back seat, 'Are we there yet!? Are we there yet!?'

No, we are not there yet. So, sit down and shut up and drink your juice but if you spill it I'll kill you and stop hitting your sister … There's still another type of energy down the road that we have to look at. Happily, it is the silliest type of energy of them all, because it's not really a real form of energy at all, It's still important, though.

We have to explore potential energy.

Did any of your teachers ever write in your report card, 'He-she has potential'? What the ?!"!/$% does that mean?

Well, I'll tell you exactly what it means. It exactly means that even though you could have done a special thing but decided not to, and the special thing that you could have done but didn't do didn't get done by you, everybody knows that if you had decided to do that special thing, it would have gotten done by you. So, whether or not you decide to do the thing or not, and whether or not the thing actually gets done by you or not, and whether or not you decide to do it or not, and whether or not it got done or not, if it had gotten done then you are the guy who would have gotten it done, Or not. Got it? OK, we're done.

That's potential. The thing that you are able to do, but haven't actually done yet. (Once you've actually done it, it becomes a feat or an accomplishment or a victory, and stops being a potential thing, since it is now done and no longer not-done.)

So potential energy is energy that does … absolutely nothing!

The best example of potential energy is a big rock sitting at the top of a big hill. Rocks don't move around a lot by themselves and they don't seem to contain any energy at all. But what if I push this rock over the hill, and let it roll down? I might just as well have unleashed a demon-possessed bulldozer. The boulder will roll down the hill, bowling over trees, houses, cars and people as if they were skittles. (Not candy skittles, the other kind.) It will not stop until it comes to rest in a place where the ground is even enough to stop its crazy roll. That stupid rock, sitting on top of his hill, hung on to his potential energy, maybe for thousands of years, until I kicked him over the side and his potential energy was released.

So potential energy is energy that is doing absolutely nothing right now, thank you very much, but call me in a week or an eon or so and we'll talk. Potential energy is energy on holiday, energy on a retirement pension. Energy playing golf in Florida. You want more metaphors, go get your own; I'm all out.

PLANKS

I LIKE PLANKS.

I met Max at the hardware the other day. He was carrying a plank. Looked like white pine, one by six by eight feet. Seemed like the only item on his list.

I was carrying a Zip-Lok baggie of O-rings and a bucket of grout. Not the pre-mixed, pre-sanded stuff; that shit is way too expensive. Just the ordinary peoples' grout for me.

"Hey, Max. Nice plank," I said.

"Sez you," he replied, disgruntled. "I went through the entire fuckn' stack, it was the least warped of the lot. Still got knots, though."

He held it up at arm's length like a rifle, which seemed a little risky in the aisles of the store, and stared one-eyed down the eight-foot edge to verify his statement. I hastily picked up the other end, and eyeballed him back. The wood felt damp and fresh, it smelled of rain and resin.

"It's pretty straight," I said. "If you nail it down soon, it'll be OK."

Max stared at me as if I had just bitten off his nose. "The knots will warp it all to hell, I'll have to plane it down. Used to be, a pine plank had no knots. If you wanted knots, you had to pay extra. Knotty pine, they called it. Faggots and rich bitches used to buy it up by the ton; they used it to decorate their summer homes. The rest of us just chopped it up for kindling. Now you can't even buy a single plank without knots."

There was a pregnant pause. I broke the silence.

"So, Max, what'll a plank like that set you back these days?"

"Eight fifty, plus tax. Four years ago, I bought the same damn plank for five bucks, and it had fewer knots, and they were bigger too. And a one-by-six measured seven-eighths by five-and-three-quarters, instead of five-eighths-by-five-and-a-quarter. So, the price is higher, the volume is reduced, and the quality is in the toilet."

"OK. So, what exactly are you going to do with that plank, Max?"

"Oh, it's just to kindle the fireplace."

DEAD WOOD

Louis Jacques was a genius, an inveterate alcoholic, and a friend of mine. He hanged himself in his basement at the age of 44. His own father had done the same.

I remember Louis crossing the street in a blistering blizzard at 8 AM completely naked except for a bath towel around his waist, to buy four 2-litre bottles of plonk from the Chinese convenience store.

"No sell! No sell!" the old Chinese lady behind the counter yelled. "You drunk! You go home! No sell to you!"

He just dumped two twenties on the counter, and said, "Gimme the change later, or keep it. I don't give a shit." Then he came back with eight litres of bad wine for our breakfast.

He picked up a screwdriver from the kitchen table, and shoved the cork down into the bottle. He chugged on the bottle for a half-minute or so, then wiped his red-stained mouth on his naked forearm and handed the bottle to me.

"Your turn," he said. The two-litre bottle was almost half-empty.

He went to the bathroom, threw up wine and blood for about two minutes, and then voided his bowels. More blood and last night's wine. He emerged and stabbed open another bottle, chugged on it.

We had been together in his apartment since the day before, and aside from a two-hour comatose nap, the pattern had been the same. Drink, drink, drink, plonk plonk plonk, chug chug chug. No glasses were ever harmed.

Louis worked for a very wealthy land owner in Old Montreal. The man owned properties that held the first buildings from the period of colonisation, over three hundred years ago. The structures were heritage sites, still intact, but they required renovation, and they had to be rebuilt EXACTLY the way that they had been erected originally, using the same tools and materials. The only man in Quebec who could do that was Louis Jacques.

One day he received a shipment of lumber from the United States. It consisted of two rough-cut timbers of white oak, 10" x 10" x 40 feet. Each beam cost $4000, and weighed about twelve hundred pounds. Louis leaned over and brushed his cheek against the moist wood, eyes closed, and breathed in the smell of it. He caressed the surface like a lover. Then he emerged from his reverie and said, "With these puppies, you measure twice, but you only cut once!"

Louis loved wood, and he could identify any piece, eyes closed, just by its weight, the texture, the sound, and the smell. "That's white pine, but not from Canada. The grain is too fine. Probably from Oregon or Washington. They've got some amazing trees. And it's fresh, probably cut six months ago. This piece is red oak, but it's more than forty years old. It's been painted at least once. Probably from Michigan or Ontario." HE WAS RIGHT EVERY TIME.

Louis worked one or two days a week. The rest of the time he lived in an alcoholic stupor that defies the imagination. He dreamed of building his own house in the Gaspésie, on the banks of the Saint Lawrence River, surrounded by the living trees that he loved so dearly. One day he quit his job, left his apartment and disappeared. Six months later, we heard the news.

When you have to chug-a-lug a two-litre bottle of plonk and then shit and vomit your own blood just to start off your day, chances are that you won't live very long. Even if you are a fucking genius.

HALLOWEEN

I LIKE HALLOWEEN.

Halloween is THE children's' event. In their eyes, it's bigger than Christmas.

Adults think that it's all about the candy, but kids know better. The candy is a perk, but the real scary fun is crossing the line. What line? The one between here and there.

The word is a smoosh of All Hallows Eve, or the evening before All Saints' Day, November 1st. It was an attempt by early evangelists to sacralise ancient pagan beliefs. Our pre-Christian ancestors lived in a world that was fragmented into multiple layers of simultaneous existence. The sky, the earth and the water were all translucid veils that separated different but equally real worlds from one another, and once a year, on or about the 1st of November, the barriers wore thin and the inhabitants of the different worlds could break through and mix and mingle like some apocalyptic cocktail party.

Some encounters were joyous, like meeting up with dead Grandma or a benevolent angel, but others were less so. Disgruntled nasty dead people or ill-intentioned demons from hell could come back to threaten you with harm, and the best way to deal with that was to offer them a sweet gift so that they would leave you alone.

This year, 2019, they postponed Halloween because the weather was bad. It was windy and rainy. The kids were champing at the bit, raring to go, the pedal to the metal, but it was the adults who chickened out and pulled the plug.

Guess what, pilgrims? That's the WHOLE POINT. Halloween is supposed to be scary. That's why kids love it. It's the beginning of winter, and it's dark and windy and cold and rainy and nature is dying, and we have designated one day out of the calendar to allow disgruntled dead people and evil hell-bent demons to return to earth and complain about why they don't really want to be dead.

We give them candy to shut them up and send them back to purgatory until next year, when they get to complain again. We've been doing that since the Stone Age, when children fought off wild predators with their bare hands and slept in dirt holes next to the skin-clad bones of their dead grandparents.

When I was a kid, our parents just threw an old sheet over us, cut out some eye holes, and kicked us out the door. There was no adult supervision whatsoever, so the offspring just lumped together willy-nilly and wandered from house to house. Often there was just one old pillowcase to carry the loot for three or more sugar-starved juvenile mendicants.

And more often than not, some teenagers would show up and kick the shit out of us and steal all of our candy. We would typically fight back, and the abundance would spill out onto the frozen sidewalk, and afterwards we would split up the leftovers before slinking back home. Usually in the pouring rain, but occasionally in snow. Without safety goggles or helmets or reflective clothing, or any adult supervision whatsoever.

Nobody spent billions of dollars on decorations or costumes. If the lights were on in the house, there was candy. Otherwise, skip to the next house.

Only rich people had jack-o'-lanterns, because pumpkins were actually food, and if you stick a candle in there you can't eat it afterwards because it will taste like wax.

Do I long for the golden days of yore? No, of course not. It was bloody hell. But we learned important life skills, like sticking up for ourselves and protecting our younger siblings without constantly running to a higher authority to settle our own petty disputes. We duked it out and skinned our knees and bloodied our elbows, and gave and got fat lips and black eyes and chipped teeth and sometimes we won and sometimes we lost. Life wasn't always fair, and we got that.

A handful of candies scattered over the cold, wet sidewalk. A torn pillowcase. A violent teenager, a toddler crying, and a frightened eight-year-old, cold and shivering, raising his fist between the two. It is precisely at this point that the seeds of heroism, altruism and self-sacrifice are conceived.

But nobody believes in that fairy tale anymore. Kids have to be bubble-wrapped until they're, like, forty years old, and anyone who dares to burst their precious bubble should be imprisoned for life.

Maybe life should ALWAYS be fair, and when it isn't, then somebody has to pay. Of course, if you are the person paying, then maybe you could argue that that's not fair, and so somebody else should pay, and so on to infinity.

And that's pretty scary.

REDEMPTION

I LIKE REDEMPTION.

When I was in grade nine, we had an English teacher who was old and fat and smelly and boring. To her credit, she not only had to teach us basic skills like spelling, grammar and syntax, but was also mandated to help us appreciate literature.

Once she required us to find a poem about travel, and read it aloud to the class. I was the only student who actually found one, and it was "The Road Not Taken" by Robert Frost, which had little to do with travel but a lot to do with life. That one flew over everybody's head, including mine, but I got credit for being the only student in the class who actually found a poem that had the word "road" in the title. She might just as well have asked us to find and read a poem about socks.

Another assignment was to write a story based on a THEME. The point, obviously, was to make us understand what a THEME was. Good luck. She actually had to provide us with a list of possible THEMES that we could use. She could just as well have handed out particles of antimatter and told us to go build a faster-than-light spacecraft.

Some of the themes she mentioned were of the like, man against man, or man against nature. (We had read *The Lord of the Flies* and *The Old Man and the Sea.*) Still, absolutely not a one of us understood what a THEME was, but I kind of picked up from the list the idea of something versus some other thing, like two things opposed.

So, I imagined a story in which a person had to make a choice between two options, neither of which was particularly desirable. In my story, a young woman suffering from tuberculosis had to swim the English Channel to earn the prize money to pay for her treatment. Since my adolescent mind could not resolve the outcome, my story simply had the woman sitting on the chilly, windswept shore, the day before the event, horking her bloody lungs up and trying to decide what to do. I do not remember what marks I got for my effort, but I suspect that I got some just for having taken the time to scribble a few incomprehensible words onto a few sheets of foolscap.

Intellectual laziness prevented me from going any further than that, but if you think about it, how many outcomes to this story are there? Either she swims, or she doesn't. If she swims, she either drowns or makes it but her condition is so bad that she dies with the prize money in her hand or she survives and gets better. If she chickens out and stays home, she simply horks her bloody lungs out and dies, or some miracle occurs, or Prince Charming storms on to the scene and sweeps her away. Deus ex Machina.

Personally, I was disappointed with my own story because it did not have a clear and fixed ending; it concluded rather ambiguously. In fact, I was incapable of deciding the fate of the imaginary person that I had created, and I felt that ultimately her destiny was pretty much up to her own imaginary self.

Life goes on. Forty years later, the THEME thing still sticks to me. You could even say that the THEME of this story is THEMES. What the hell are they? I dunno. But since then I have watched a lot of movies and read a lot of books. That does not make me a smart person or a wise person, but it gives me a good idea of what book-writers and movie-makers use as THEMES.

Funny now that you mention it, in my story about the channel-swimming girl with tuberculosis, I was initially inspired by a conflictual dichotomy. A what who when now you say? It sounds complicated, but it is probably the most fundamental principal in art and literature. Opposites that are in direct conflict, and only one can win, but they never actually do, or only do so temporarily, otherwise the story would end there and then we would be bored to tears for eternity. The good guys in white hats who always face right versus the bad guys in black hats who always turn to the left.

This is opposed to complementary dichotomy, in which opposites are required to fill a void; their opposing forces act like a battery that is required to dynamize the universe. Hot and cold, left and right, up and down, good and bad, light and dark, life and death, night and day, male and female, positive and negative, sun and moon, joy and sorrow, youth and old age, and you could fill a planet full of libraries with other examples. (We can save trichotomies for another time and planet.)

So that creates a dichotomy of dichotomies; i.e., opposites that are mutually exclusive versus opposites that are mutually dependent. Can we call that a quadrotomy? Eew. I think not.

So, go watch a movie or a TV show or read a book. In every instance, there are ALWAYS good guys and bad guys, although sometimes it is hard to tell the difference because the story-teller is trying to tell both sides of the story at the same time, or trying to tell the story from the point of view of the people that everybody has already decided are the bad guys, or sometimes good people do bad things and versa visa..

My old, fat smelly English teacher had a list of possible themes for us adolescent morons. The problem was that the list was too long. There is, in fact, only one fundamental theme in all music, art, cinema and literature, and it can be resolved in a single word: REDEMPTION.

It is a word. Look it up. It basically means getting back something precious that you have lost or never owned. (You will notice that I do not use contractions and it is because I cannot find the apostrophe on my new keyboard.)

The simplest interpretation of the REDEMPTION theme is REVENGE. The downtrodden kick the asses of their evil oppressors. Charlie Chaplin, Mickey Mouse, Clint Eastwood, Homer, Dante, Shakespeare, Molière, Dickens, Dumas Père et Fils, Bruce Willis, Donkey Kong and you can fill this list to infinity. This theme so satisfies people's appetites that it dominates the majority of popular media. Most of the classic operas mine this quarry to the last grain of sand.

We have all been victims of other people's selfishness and the desire to hit back is always inside of us. Most of us do not react to our primal impulses, because usually they have severe social, moral, and legal consequences. But the movies can smack back hard at our collectively perceived aggressors and give us a sense of personal collective justice.

But if vengeance is one of the most popular themes in popular culture, it is also the basest, easiest and most simplistic. Whacking your adversary upside the head with a two-by-four because he done you wrong certainly will satisfy your immediate sense of personal justice, but not only is it ex-legal vigilante terrorism and behaving exactly like you did not want them to do to you in the first place, it also lacks a certain dignity.

REDEMPTION. You were in a nice place before some shit happened and it was either your fault or somebody else's fault or nobody's fault but either way you are not in a nice place any more and you have to either kick some ass to go back to the nice place and win or fail, or lie down and die, or a hero will come and rescue you.

Read that last line again. It describes, in one sentence, absolutely EVERY STORY EVER TOLD from the Stone Age to today's NYT best-sellers list. There are no other possible story lines. Adam and Eve, Hansel and Gretel, Homer and Shakespeare and Dante and Mao Tse-Tung and Hollywood, the *Iliad* and *Star Wars* and *The Lord of the Rings* and *The Good The Bad And The Ugly* and EVERY OTHER ATTEMPT TO TELL A STORY FROM CAVEMEN TO THE PRESENT must absolutely conform to that definition. If you can find a single exception in the entire inventory of human literature, I will roll over and die, after eating my own head. Boiled, baked or stir-fried, your choice. If you can create a story that defies this definition, I can guarantee that it will be banal. (Jokes excluded.)

Jokes are excluded because they are literary weeds. They break the rules by growing where you don't want them to and generally disrupting what we perceive to be order and convention. And no matter how hard we try to control them, they just keep on cropping up and defying our definition of what is right and orderly.

But they feed the bees and the butterflies, and so we endure them. We may even enjoy and foster them, though without ever admitting it.

DEATH

I LIKE DEATH.

There's nothing wrong with being dead. I know lots of dead people, and few of them ever complain. Well, not much.

The problem is not with being dead, but with actually getting dead. The bridge, the temporal transition between total absolute health and stone-cold annihilation. That's the bitch.

The only people who ever complain are those that sit on the bridge, incapable of turning back, but unwilling to move forward. That's absolutely everybody.

The drowning person has only a few seconds to make their peace; the cancer victim may have several years. The result is the same. Fresh-cut flowers spread over a fresh-dug hole in the ground. It is our collective destiny. To pretend otherwise is to deny the beautiful gift that we have all been offered.

From my putrid flesh flowers will grow, and I will be among them. And that, my friend, is eternity!

That last quote is from Edvard Munch, whose main claim to fame is that he was, by his own admission, simultaneously afflicted with the two worst curses of mankind, poverty and mental illness.

Getting dead is as real and as glorious and as scary as getting born, and between those two inevitable events some crazy shit happens that turns us into real people. Each one of us has a moment to interact with the physical universe before we are brushed aside in favor of another, for better or worse.

And then we advance to, or return to, a place where the universal physical laws no longer apply. Physicists call that a singularity. A black hole. The instant before the big bang. The momentary space just beyond the observable universe. The infinite time in which a photon exists.

I'm not scared of that. If I wasn't so caught up with my own fingers and my eyes and my nose and my ears and my tongue and my penis I would have fled to that sweet refuge long ago. Having been there once, I know exactly what to expect. A decent night's sleep, for once in my life, with no alarm clock at the other end, except maybe the Angel Gabriel's bloody horn blasting in my ear like a demented sergeant major calling the dead man's reveille, urging all of us to either heaven or hell depending on our paperwork.

Baptized Lutheran? Eew. Baptist? Seriously? No fucking way! Don't let the name fool you! Eastern orthodox? Maybe. How many indulgences did you buy? Register all of your invoices over there; Saint Peter will be glad to tote them up for you. Hold on! Purchasing indulgences with cash money is a sin! You have to earn them through acts of contrition, charity and self-sacrifice! OK. Giving your money to the church rather than keeping it selfishly for yourself pretty much fulfills all of those conditions, not?

Forgot to confess your sins on your deathbed? Your file is pending; please take a number and wait out in the hall. Posthumous baptism? Not usually allowed, but we'll check the credentials and get back to you. You can't get in if you ain't baptized, but if it happened after you died, you didn't really consent, did you? Or you missed the deadline.

Incoming! Infant new-born baby. Are you properly baptized? Sho'nuff, I'm still all nekked and wet. Did you renounce Satan? Of course not, you moron. I'm a new-born fuckn' baby. My godfather did that for me. Was he sincere? How the fuck should I know? I barely know the old bastard. Isn't it your job to read people's minds? OK then, off you go. Next?

Uh-oh. Multiple baptisms. This one's a dilemma.

Lemme see now. This document has you baptized Lutheran at birth.

Yeah, so? L'ill baby Jesus and Saint Peter are bent over their desks, carefully scrutinizing the precious parchment.

It looks legal; the signature of the parish priest has been authenticated by our archivists.

So, what's the problem?

Well, Saint Peter answers, looking mighty grave, had this document been signed in, say, 1750, when protestants like yourself were considered Satan worshipers, we would have had to send you straight to hell. Had we caught you before you died, we would have been obliged to burn you alive first, and then send you straight to hell.

And so, what's the problem?

Ha ha, Baby Jesus chimed in, adding a bit of levity to the interview. Since then, we've, you know, reconciled a few of our differences with the, um, you know, some of the, uh, various offshoots of the one true orthodox church.

What, the protestants?

Yes, precisely. The, um, protestants. We are, after all, a church of peace, harmony, and understanding. Unless you disagree with us, in which case we have no other option than to brutally torture and kill you. But merely as a disincentive to other potential dissenters, you understand. A mere formality. Nothing personal.

OK. So why am I here? My paperwork is in order.

Well yes, in fact the Lutherans are one of the, um, you know, one of the so-called rebellious sects with whom we have been able to negotiate a truce. Their documents are indeed recognized as legitimate by our council. Your baptism certificate, in principle, should allow you into heaven.

In principle? What's the hang-up? Why am I still here talking to you?

That's when Saint Peter stood up and cleared his stately throat.

Ahem. I have before me another document. It is a baptism certificate from Verdun Baptist Church dated December the 11th 1974, with your name on it, when you were sixteen years old.

Uncle Pete slammed the document down and pointed an accusing finger.

Do you deny that you were baptised at this time and in this heathen place?

No, of course not. They told me that my relationship with the One True God had to be based on mutual consent and that only an adult with a true understanding of the importance of the commitment and with free will can participate in the Holy Sacrament of baptism.

What else did these heretics teach you?

That baptizing babies was a stupid outdated Medieval ritual that dated to a time when most babies died during or shortly after childbirth, and that baptizing them as infants was the only way to get them to heaven, but the consent had to be given by an adult who assumed their sins because new-born babies are incapable of confessing because, well, they are babies.

Saint Pete and bearded old Baby Jesus looked at each other, gravely shaking their heads. Then they turned to me and broke the news.

You understand, Mr. Sapin, that in order to get to heaven you have to be properly baptized. There is no other way. Your initial baptism as a baby in the Lutheran church would have sufficed to allow you entry, but your subsequent baptism in a heathen church implies a complete and total voluntary renunciation of your original baptism, so as far as we are concerned, the second baptism cancels out the first one, and you have never ever been baptized at all. So, you can't come in. The two smug bastards sat there across the table from me, arms crossed and eyes bent.

And so I did what any sane person would do confronted by such insensitive, brutalizing divine bureaucracy. I stood up and leaned over the table and grabbed Saint Pete by his long black stately beard and smashed my fist into his pompous face over and over again until he was pissing blood from every orifice, and then I tipped over the table, spilling the sacrosanct documents all over the cloudy floor, and grabbed a broken, nail-studded chair leg and brutally beat the li'll white-bearded baby Jesus unconscious upside the head, allowing him a brief respite as he turned the other cheek, then added a few new stigmata to his face. I then strode over and past their two inert, bruised, bleeding and broken bodies right up to the pearly gates, where the Angels Michael and Gabriel greeted me with outstretched wings and they said, thank you, Unca Dave. It's about time somebody put those two self-righteous pricks in their place.

As Dumas Père once wrote, you only die once, but then for such a long, long time.

But living people expect signed documents, hard copy in triplicate, notaries, lawyers, witnesses, official stamps and seals, *et al.* And absolutely everyone expects to live forever. Call it denial, or cognitive dissonance, but without it none of us would ever get out of bed in the morning.

So, help me with this paperwork, please.

Unca Dave

TEARS

I LIKE CRYING.

The fact is, I almost never cry. I didn't cry when my dad died, nor my mom. I'll shed a boatload of tears when I cut up a fresh onion, but that's about it. In fact, I could actually accidentally lop off my thumb, and that would generate some pain and maybe a bit of anxiety, but it won't make me cry.

I would probably just bend over and pick it up, then carry it to the kitchen sink where I would run it and the bleeding stump under cold water for a few minutes, until my nosy wife would come along and ask me what I'm doing.

"What you got there?"

"It's my thumb."

"What's it doing in the kitchen sink?"

"I cut it off."

"What the hell for?"

"I dunno. It just sort of, you know, came off while I was chopping wood. Never saw it coming."

"You want I take you to the emergency?"

"I dunno. How long's the wait time? I have to work tomorrow. Got any Tylenol? Extra-strength would be nice."

"You're not gonna get much work done without your thumb."

"Fer Pete's sake, I still have the other one!"

But no tears. The fact is, I have an unusually high pain

threshold. Part of it stems from the fact that, when I was nine years old, my dad sent me to the dentist because I had really bad cavities in all of my front teeth. It's some kind of hereditary thing. He specifically told the dentist not to give me any pain killers, so I got all eight front teeth drilled right down to the nerve from both sides and from the back, each without the benefit of novocaine, just like Dustin Hoffman in Marathon Man. Of course, he was merely acting the part. I got to do the real thing.

Since I was only nine years old, I didn't know any better and I just assumed that that was how it was supposed to be when you went to the dentist. My dad thought that the whole thing was totally hilarious, like some kind of cute, harmless April Fool's joke, and he probably also got a discount on the dentist's bill. But ever since then my brain has been hard-wired to override even the most excruciating agony that you can imagine. The Spanish Inquisition would have met their match with me, and I am still debating in my mind whether or not that is a good thing.

Now here's the irony. Yesterday I was farting around in the basement, not doing anything dangerous with power tools. Just sorting out a big box full of used screws and nails and washers and hinges and other rusty old crap, listening to the radio. You can actually get tetanus or hepatitis or golden staph from doing that. (No, not from listening to the radio, but from playing with filth-encrusted vintage hardware, so kids, don't try this at home!)

And then the song came on.

It was one of those radio stations that I like to call "ketchup."

Most radio stations pick a theme and then play the same tired old songs over and over and over and over. They call it "heavy rotation" and it's about as much fun as it sounds.

I like to listen to the same songs over and over and over again. But I prefer to pick the songs myself, rather than have an over-paid DJ impose them on me. A few years ago, I played Abba's

"Waterloo" on my turntable at least sixty times non-stop, because I was trying to figure out the lyrics, and when they sang: "I was defeated, you won the war," all I heard was, "I was just feeding you wonderwall." Sixty times over. Maybe more; I wasn't actually keeping score. Back then we didn't have the benefit of Google, so if the album didn't come with liner notes, the only way to figure out the words was to listen to the song over and over and over and over and over and …

Since that made no sense to me whatsoever, I simply wrote it down as: "I was just feeding you guacamole," and even though that was obviously dead wrong, at least I knew that "guacamole," being a sort of food, made more sense than "wonderwall," which probably wasn't.

To be fair, I was only playing Abba because I was acting as host to a bunch of wild mice that had invaded my home, and I didn't have the heart to kill them, so I invented a humanitarian trap to catch them alive, but since it was the dead of winter I had to build a vivarium to keep them in until spring.

Meanwhile, I had opened a box of old vinyl records that I had bought the previous summer at a garage sale without ever investigating the contents. Apparently, the previous owner was a big Abba fan. I had never been much of a fan personally; when they were popular I was heavily rotating on Johnny Rotten and Joey Ramone.

I like buying old vinyl LPs, but I stopped rummaging through the crates years ago and now I just buy the whole box and sort them out at home, which is why I now have, like, nine copies of Carol King's "Tapestry," at least six of Michael Jackson's "Thriller" and I stopped counting the copies of Pink Floyd's "Dark Side of the Moon" years ago. (That's not actually the title of the album, but everybody calls it that and we all know exactly which one we mean.) I also have an impressive collection of K-Tel non-stop disco party compilations, as advertised on TV.

But I noticed that when I started playing Abba, the mice seemed more relaxed and happier. They crawled out of their hidey-holes and gleefully played on the impromptu toys that I had thrown together for their enjoyment.

So, I figured, if it's good for the mice, maybe it's good for me. I played Abba non-stop until my wife threatened me with a divorce. In retrospect, I can't say that I blame her. Too much of a good thing will kill you, unless you are a mouse.

I switched back to listening to a local radio station. I don't remember which one, but I called it ketchup, because when you make homemade ketchup, you don't really care about the ingredients. You just toss whatever left-over overripe fruit and spoiled vegetables you've got into the pot with some sugar and water and vinegar and spices, boil it all up, and voila! Delicious, nutritious homemade ketchup! So, this radio station treated me to everything from big-band jazz to bagpipes, opera to old show tunes, and even the mice seemed to enjoy it all.

But then, as I mentioned, something happened. A song came on that I had not heard in thirty years.

It was Dorothy Moore singing "Misty Blue." And I suddenly dropped what I was doing and burst into tears. Not just a trickle, or even a small flood, but a goddam tidal wave. A fucking tsunami. An apocalyptic hurricane. A triple-mop cleanup job.

Such is the power of art. You should listen to that song some time, if you ever get the chance. Even if it doesn't make you cry, if you are at all even remotely human, it should at least nibble your ass.

Just make sure you get your tetanus shot afterwards. Some music is infectious.

BOOKS

I LIKE BOOKS. I grew up with books. My mother read them to me until we were both red-eyed and eventually I was able to read them by myself.

In a world without Google or smart phones or cable TV, books were the only way to learn about anything, unless you actually had to talk to old people, which nobody ever wanted to do ever. And you typically didn't find books on a park bench. You bought them, if you were very wealthy, but otherwise you had to go to the library.

So last Saturday I was farting around in the basement, pretending to do something useful, when I came upon a book. Actually, it was a pile of very old stinky books, but one in particular stood out.

Most of all because it was huge, by modern standards. It weighs five pounds. It looked like a very old dictionary. The stiff hard cover was dark green, almost black, and smelled of mould and glue and dead flies, and was bereft of any inscriptions whatsoever, except for a tiny gold imprint on the two-inch spine.

A Conrad Argosy. Underlined by a simple, curly golden doodle. There is absolutely no other information about the book anywhere on the hard, stiff outside.

I casually flipped through the first few pages. This edition was published By Doubleday, Doran and Company, Inc., in Garden City, New York in 1942, but the first copyright is from 1897.

I read the three-page introduction. Here's the Reader's Digest version:

Joseph Conrad was born in Russian Poland in 1857 of a noble family, although low on the totem pole. Briefly, all of his family was exterminated by czarist forces and as an exile he joined the British merchant marines and made a career as a pirate, smuggler and gunrunner. He learned to speak English at the age of twenty.

Fifteen years later he put pen to paper for the first time in his life, and after many other tribulations, went on to be considered one of the greatest literary geniuses that the British Empire had ever produced.

That struck me as a bit of hyperbole, so I shut the book and went to bed.

The next morning, I got up and had my coffee, and the stinky old book was still sitting on the kitchen table where I had left it the night before, and it was inevitable and unavoidable by its sheer size and overpowering aroma, so I decided to put it to the test.

I flipped it open at random, all seven hundred pages, the way that evangelical bible revivalists do when they are seeking divine prophetic revelation, and began to read the first thing that I saw. After perusing only two pages, I had tears in my eyes. My wife rushed to my side, thinking that I had injured myself. Maybe I had.

It's OK, I reassured her, sobbing, wiping my snotty nose on my sleeve like a child. It's only a stinky old book …

But it wasn't the dust and mould that made me sniff and cry. It was the words on the page. I won't quote any, partly because I'm lazy, but also because I want to avoid copyright infringement issues. And also, because I will leave you to discover this literary treasure all by yourself, if you haven't already. Any one of those seven hundred pages will grip your heart in a full nelson, if you have one at all.

A Polish immigrant fleeing the czarist pogroms that decimated his family becomes a swashbuckling, sabre-swinging career pirate, learns English, which doesn't even use the same alphabet, and then goes on to become a literary icon. You might see that in the movies and think to yourself, sheesh. What other outrageous incongruous impossible unbelievable bullshit will they dream up next?

If you ever get a chance to read Joseph Conrad, I strongly encourage you to do so.

Otherwise, maybe I can lend you the stinky old book. Either way, you're gonna cry.

TATTOOS AND CHANDELIERS

FORTY-SIX MILLION DOLLARS.

Not for the house, or the terrain.

Just for the chandeliers Inside the house, sitting on the terrain. They're made of solid gold.

Meanwhile, his citizens are starving to death in the Streets of Kiev.

It's called Mezhyhiria, and it's the personal residence of Viktor Yanukovich, the former president of the Ukraine, and the whole shitwad (property, buildings and furnishings) is valued at about forty billion dollars US, or about one-third of the country's annual GDP. For that kind of money you could probably buy most of Beverly Hills and still have enough left over for a deposit on Malibu.

As president, the man had a declared income of about two thousand dollars a month. Even I make more than that, and I get my lamps from Ikea. All the rest is the fruit of unabashed corruption.

One would think that the Ukrainians would have thrown over that yoke after Red October in 1917. They murdered the Tsar and his ministers for precisely the same reason. Apparently, Anastasia screamed in vain.

Ukraine. The bread basket of the Soviet Union. In 1932, Joseph Stalin bragged about record wheat harvests in the Ukraine thanks to his collective farms and five-year plans. That same year, SEVEN MILLION Ukrainian peasants starved to death while harvesting his bumper crop. They could grow it, but were forbidden to eat it. They couldn't even pick the few mouldy old fallen grains out of the mud under penalty of death.

1944. Another FIVE MILLION Ukrainians lost their lives fighting the Nazis. Many were civilians, including women and children, armed only with farm implements.

The numbers are staggering. That's TWELVE MILLION dead in under two decades. Most Ukrainians remember. How could you forget?

Yanukovich. What a fat pig. When the Ukes get hold of him, I would love to be there for the barbecue. They are gonna shove that red-hot steel skewer right up his ass until it comes out of his mouth, then turn him slowly over a nice hot fire until the flesh drops from his bones. While he's still alive. Maybe they'll shove a ripe red apple in his mouth, if they can find one.

But that won't happen.

He scurried off to Moscow, crying on Poutine's shoulder. Once he transfers his personal fortune to a bank in Moscow, and then to London and eventually to Liechtenstein, he will disappear from the map forever. It's either sailing in the Caymans or a bullet between the eyes and an unmarked grave, depending on how the negotiations go over there. But I guess a quick death is better than Stalin's preferred means of dealing with ministers that he disliked. Piano wire or a meat hook.

Either way, he is retired from the political scene for a bit, although rumour has it that after being ousted from power and buggering off out the back door, he's building another, more luxurious mansion on the shore of the Black Sea.

Why do I care? I dunno. Maybe I'd like to live in a world where people stop shitting on each other, not merely for wealth and power, but for conspicuous luxury. Seems to me that there's enough to go around, as long as you don't put a priority on forty-six million dollar solid-gold chandeliers, and you have to shoot ordinary people in the head and kill them dead or starve them to death in order to obtain them.

Most Ukrainians are not ethnic Russians. They are of Scandinavian descent, more Viking, tall and blonde, than Slavic, swarthy and stumpy. More Volvo than Lada, as it were.

There was a nice Ukrainian girl at my high school whose name I have totally forgotten. Nope. Maryanne. Her name was Maryanne. We were good friends until one day she forgot to do up the last button on her blouse and I got a glimpse of the top of her bra and a really teeny weeny tiny bit of cleavage. After that we were so mutually embarrassed, every time we met we turned beet red and stomped off in opposite directions.

I was only twelve years old at the time, and I wouldn't have any pubic hair for another four years. Still, a bit of teen angst sure beats fighting off an organized army of armed soldiers with a shovel. Her family had gone there, did that. Ho hum.

Fast forward about a decade. Back in the eighties, I worked in a design studio on Queen Street West, in Toronto. Across the street was a convenience store where we bought our potato chips, cigarettes and candy bars.

The owner was an old man, dried-up, impatient, irascible and unpleasant. Everybody hated him. He barely spoke English, but he could curse like the best of them.

One day, as he handed me my change, his shirtsleeve accidentally slid up on his forearm, and I saw it. The tattooed number. A survivor of the damn fucking Holocaust. Auschwitz? Birkenau? Spandau? I dunno. Not a subject of conversation. You finished? OK. Get the fuck outa my store before I call the fuckin' cops. You gonna buy that pack of gum or fondle it till it melts? This ain't a fuckin' Library; buy the fuckin' magazine or put it back! Choose yer ice cream bar BEFORE you open the freezer, idiot!

Needless to say, I doubt if he sold many franchises. But that gangrene-coloured tattoo is burned onto my brain as permanently and as indelibly as the original was onto that man's shrivelled arm.

People will continue to destroy one another to acquire what they desire, just as they have always done. There's enough chewing gum for the entire class, and afterwards we could all have a nap, and then we could all play nice and share our toys and have a snack.

Unless you absolutely have to have a forty-six-million-dollar solid gold chandelier, in which case we will all haul out our handguns and shoot to kill. Last one standing takes everyone else's milk carton and cookies. All agreed? Boom boom boom boom. Shit. All of the milk cartons have bullet holes in them. Most of the people too. Any cookies left? Any without blood and guts on them? Where's my goddamned solid gold chandelier?

Ironically, this outrageously obscene accumulation of ostentatious wealth is precisely the motivation that has enabled the greatest works of art and engineering that humanity has ever achieved. The Giza pyramids. The Parthenon. Saint Peter's Basilica. Notre Dame de Paris. Stonehenge. Canterbury Cathedral. The Great Wall of China. Angor Vat. Chichen Itza.

We admire and venerate all of those places, and consider them sacred pilgrimage destinations.

Go figure.

JAIL

I LIKE JAIL.

I've been to jail, where I've had to defend myself against men twice my size, and with a fraction of my moral sense of what is right or wrong. I've been locked up in the looney bin, where I was under the care of the same doctors who had performed illegal clandestine drug experiments on American soldiers. I have also eaten out of dumpsters and worn the same clothes without ever removing a single piece for an entire winter, and when the T-shirt finally came off, the rotten black skin on my back peeled off with it. We had to burn my entire wardrobe, right down to the shit-encrusted skivvies.

I won't go back there, but I won't piss and whine about how life dealt me the two of clubs. My stories are borne out of those experiences, and I wouldn't trade any of those real-life adventures for any ten-thousand-dollar luxury cruise to anywhere.

I was bullied as a child. We all were, every one of us, at some point, to lesser or greater degrees. Eddie would stalk me after school and push me down on the sidewalk and sit on my back and repeatedly smash my face into the concrete pavement every single day in broad daylight, and adults walking by would simply sidestep us and allow us our childish pranks.

Back then, it was just part of the growing-up ritual. All anyone ever told me was, "Stick up for yourself. Fight back, because we ain't gonna do squat." By "we" I mean every single adult around me, including my parents, my teachers, the principal, and the police. So, despite my own fear of retribution and my own third-grade better judgement, I eventually smacked my bully upside the head so hard that he squealed like a stuck pig, and cried like a little girl. Actually, I smashed his head face-first into a cast iron radiator in the stairwell at school with all the strength that I could muster. I had no other alternative, no other option. I was eight years old. After that he followed me around everywhere like a faithful puppy dog.

When I got to jail thirty years later, I ended up sitting in the cafeteria seat of a biker convicted of murder, a paid hit man for the Hell's Angels. When he showed up to claim his place, I stood up in front of two hundred inmates and five armed security guards with itchy trigger fingers, stared him straight in the eye and stabbed his nose with my index and shouted, "This seat doesn't have your name on it!"

Total silence in the dining hall. All eyes were on us. I am pointing upwards because this guy is a full head taller than me, and twice my weight. Inside, I am shitting in my pants. He can snap my neck in a second, eyes closed and one hand behind his back. Fights were routine in the cafeteria, and the guards usually held back until one or the other was ready for the infirmary. And I don't mean a black eye or a bloody nose or a chipped tooth; more like a concussion, a coma and a month in intensive care.

A few seconds of silence that felt like an eternity in a black hole, and then my adversary broke eye contact, glanced about the room, and said, "Ok for this time." He then turned away and sought another seat in the crowded cafeteria, and how many men spontaneously sprang up out of their own to accommodate him.

I sat back down in my own purloined space, and my first impulse was to just vomit all over the table from the adrenalin rush that was trying to make my head explode. My mouth was filling with acid bile, turning my stomach to stone, and forcing my bowels and bladder into emergency evacuation mode. But I just clamped my teeth together, picked up my knife and fork in hard twisted fists and pressed my forearms down against the table so hard that no one could see that my hands were shaking like palm trees in a tornado, and deliberately pressed unwanted food into my mouth in an attempt to imitate normalcy.

Panic-mode adrenalin-fired fight-or-flight spontaneous bowel effluent doesn't smell at all like normal shit.

My three table guests were as white as ice, their lower jaws pendulating like metronomes. I pretended to eat my lunch, then politely asked the others if they were going to finish their desserts. All silently declined, so I gathered them up onto my own tray, walked over to my potential foe, and silently and reverently laid them out before him. There was a fraction of a second of serious silent eye contact that sealed forever a permanent pact of mutual non-aggression and solidarity. Had I glanced away from those cold steel eyes even for an instant, my fate was sealed.

From that moment on, everyone in the prison, including the guards, called me Mister Sapin, and I was nobody's lap dog or party girl. I had publicly confronted Satan Incarnate, and He had stepped down.

Inmates offered me cigarettes and candy and everyone wanted to play checkers with me in the common room, because just sitting at the same table endowed them with a kind of supernatural indemnity from harm. I probably could have sold my hair clippings as talismans.

The bully wasn't stupid. He figured out that he was bigger and stronger when the smart kid was his ally, rather than his adversary.

I seriously shit my pants that day at the cafeteria. That momentary confrontation was one of the worst episodes of my entire life.

I certainly do not own the monopoly on hardship. We all got bruises. No exceptions. Some worse than others; it's not a competition.

But I learned that even convicted murderers are actually real people.

And I also learned that prison walls can liberate you, whereas perceived liberties can, and will, enslave you.

FROM POTATOES TO DOORKNOBS

MY MOM WAS FOURTEEN YEARS OLD when the war broke out. That's WWII, for those who keep track of that sort of stuff. Her mom had died of tuberculosis a few years before, leaving her to care for four younger siblings. She lived in Reading, which today is a suburb of London, but back then it was a village north of the bustling metropolis.

How about the day the men in the lorries came around and invaded every home? They took down every door and window in the house to extract the brass hinges and doorknobs and screws, and just left the doors and windows lying about to be chopped up for firewood to heat a doorless, windowless home.

How about when my mom worked in a biscuit factory, and the teenage girls would write secret love letters to boys and men that had so abruptly abandoned them and secretly stuffed the clandestine missives into the cookie tins? The boxes were then sent abroad to soldiers fighting all across Europe, and some of the men found the letters among the comfort food, and actually replied from the trenches. My mom had a few responses, but she complained that, when she actually sent a picture of herself, the correspondence abruptly ended.

She maintained that the servicemen found her unattractive because she had rotten teeth. Trench mouth was the official medical term. Her nickname back home was "Skagtooth Nell."

In fact, my mom had all of her teeth extracted at the tender age of sixteen due to malnutrition, just as the metal teeth from the doors and windows of her home were brutally extracted for the war effort, and the abandoned doors and windows were cast aside and the ruined façade of the house became as attractive as her own demolished, bulldozed, bombed-out, war-torn, teary-eyed teenage face.

But it seems unlikely that the soldiers who got the pictures ever saw beyond those smiling lips, thinly smeared with bright red black-market lipstick, appearing as merely another shade of grey on the grainy black-and-white photographs.

I suspect that the return mail actually stopped coming not because the poor bastards could taste or smell or see her putrid, toothless pus-infected gums from a blurry monochrome picture of a pretty girl with sad eyes and a pursed Mona Lisa smile a thousand miles away, but because they had gotten their own bloody gritting teeth blown out in some grim red-and-black-and-grey ungodly frozen pus-infected trench a thousand miles from home.

The girls and women sold their hair, which was used to insulate soldiers' boots and to stuff the seats in the tanks and airplanes. They spent the cash on black-market lipstick and stockings to seduce boys who had all left to get ripped to shreds on the battlefield. One lipstick cost a week's wages, and she had to share with five other girls, each one spreading the tiniest amount to make it last. Obviously, they couldn't choose from ninety-seven designer colors. They smoked cigarettes and rolled up the tin wrapping paper into little balls, and when they had a handful they could exchange it for a free ticket to the movies to see Humphrey Bogart and Lauren Bacall in living black-and-white and pretend for an hour or two that life was normal.

WW2. My parents had ration cards. My dad ate his neighbour's dog. Butchered it and broiled it and fed it to his siblings. It was the only meat they had in months. (He claimed that it had been hit by a streetcar.) After the cookie factory, my mom worked in a machine shop on a metal lathe churning out parts for tanks and guns, and caring for four younger siblings because her mom had died at age forty-five after popping out fourteen kids. Only one out of two of them ever got to go to school because there weren't enough shoes for everybody, and you couldn't go to school barefoot, and often the boys had to wear their sisters' girlie shoes because they were the only ones that fit.

Every night for two hundred consecutive days my mom watched the V-2 rockets explode all over London. Every time they hit, the house would tremble from the earthquake and the horizon would light up with blazing fireworks.

Government lorries would routinely drive through each neighborhood collecting metal objects for the war effort. But after a while there were no more spare spoons or plates or buckets or pots and pans or garden tools, so the men ripped up the metal gates and fences and tossed them onto their flatbeds and trundled them off to the factories to be forged into lethal weapons.

After that, all that was left were the metal hinges, locks and knobs on the doors and windows. The houses were left as toothless and vulnerable as the young women who worked in those dark, noisy, toxic factories.

Fast forward a half century. My mom and dad got to Canada and had two kids. Me and my sister. Then my sister had a kid. His name is Matti because his dad is from Finland. My dad, who was from Switzerland, bought a modest property in the Laurentians and we generally referred to it as the country house.

Today the proper nomenclature would be cottage, like cottage cheese, as if some kind of traditional crafts were executed there like weaving or macramé or wicker-work, but none of that ever happened. Shitloads of other stupid stuff occurred, but we'll save those bizarre stories for another episode.

So now my dad is dead and the remaining parts of the family are reunited at the country house. That's my mom, me, my sister Susan and her five-year-old son Matti, and his infant sister Mia. That's the entire Sapin family on this side of the Atlantic.

It's a nice summer afternoon, and all are agreed that supper will be forthcoming if everyone shares in the chores. So, my sister installs her five-year-old son Matti at the table, and he is eager to participate, so she lays out some old newspaper in front of him and gives him a sharp kitchen knife and a potato and asks him to peel it.

My mom, the kid's grandma, was absolutely mortified. Not because her daughter, her own progeny, would allow a five-year-old child to wield a sharp knife and possibly injure himself. Oh, no. That wasn't the source of anxiety. Kids are supposed to injure themselves; it builds character and shores up the immune system and prepares them for the hardships and disappointments of adult life, if they live that long.

On that level, I totally agree, and I will probably rot in hell for eternity for saying so. That wasn't the problem.

"He's going to spoil the potato!" my mom wailed.

Shit. I had to remind my own mother that the war was actually over, and had been for more than a half century, that she could turn in her ration cards, and that potatoes cost about a nickel each.

If looks could kill, I would be writing this story posthumously. But I did possess an amazing immune system, an abnormally high tolerance for pain, really cool aviator-frame mirror shades Like Peter Fonda in *Easy Rider*, and a thick blonde moo-stash, so I actually survived the maternal Evil Eye almost unscathed, like Perseus versus the Medusa.

Most of the potato was salvaged, no major injuries were reported, and a decent supper was enjoyed by all.

MILK MONEY

I LIKE COINS.

When I was eight years old, coin collecting was a respectable hobby for young boys. But how can you collect coins when each black penny could buy you a multitude of penny-candy?

We used to scour the back alleys in search of discarded glass pop bottles, each of which was worth two cents. When you had five, you could trade them in for a chocolate bar or two popsicles or a comic book or two small bags of potato chips. Or a tiny brown paper bag full of penny candy.

The candies were displayed in a child-sized glass-covered counter, the same way that your meat is displayed at a butcher shop. And you could point to the candies and pick and choose among them, and the shop owner would hand-pick them and place them in the tiny brown paper bag, one at a time.

Considering the amazing purchasing power of a single penny, there wasn't much room in the budget to put one away now and again just to stuff it into a collection.

But we managed. The game was to find at least one from every single year, and then line them up in order and see which ones were missing, and then trade them to complete the collection.

As we grew older, and our pocket-money budgets increased, we were able to extend the game to nickels, and even some dimes.

In 1972 the family flew to Switzerland. This was not a holiday. My dad was born there in 1925, and he emigrated to Canada after the war, so we were just visiting family. But I was suddenly exposed to a whole new world of coin-collecting.

Switzerland has not changed the designs on their coins since the nineteenth century, so it was not uncommon to find coins in your pocket change still in circulation that dated back to 1885. All transactions were rounded out then to the nearest 5 cents, but the old copper one and two cent coins could still be found in circulation, if you knew where to look.

The post office still accepted them, but they handed out paper stamps in lieu of coins when they owed you change. The best place to find them was at the "*laiterie*," or milk-house.

The milk business is a state-run monopoly in Switzerland. My uncle and aunt owned a summer house in the village of Berolle in the Jura. It had a permanent resident population of 136 people, and most of them were dairy farmers who owned between five and twenty cows. Each cow had a name like *Charmette* or *Marguerite* and they were lovingly hand-milked twice a day and the warm, raw milk was trundled off to the "*laiterie*," a tiny building with a concrete floor and a massive stainless-steel balance hanging from the ceiling in the middle.

Every morning and every afternoon after milking, the farmers would line up at the *laiterie* and their milk was weighed to the nearest gram in the giant balance, and they were paid in cash to the nearest copper penny by a government agent. The price of the milk was never ever rounded off to the nearest nickel, as all other transactions in the country were, so they always used the tiny old copper one and two-cent coins to complete the transaction.

Afterwards, the villagers who did not actually own cows, like us, could line up and buy milk from the giant bucket. We had to bring a *berlingot*, which was just a small plastic container with a handle and a tight-fitting lid, and the government agent would fill our container using one of a series of stainless-steel ladles hanging on the wall behind him, each with a government stamp that guaranteed perfect measurement up to the rim.

How much do you want? One litre? Off came the one-litre ladle, and filled to the brim with a steady hand, it went into your berlingot. If you paid with large coins, you might get a few copper ones back in your change, and my aunt typically let me keep those. The rest of the milk was trundled off to a factory where it eventually became butter or cheese, but by the time I got back to the house the cow-warm milk in my berlingot had separated into a solid clot of thick cream on the top and happy warm whole unpasteurized cow's milk on the bottom. Often that was the daily meal. A hot bowl of milk with bread and butter and cheese. And a few tiny brass coins in my pocket.

And I do mean tiny. The one-centime coin is smaller than your pinkie nail. If you dropped one on thc lawn, it would be lost forever. Compare that to a contemporary British one-penny coin, which was almost the size of your fist. If you had ten of those in your pocket, you would need suspenders and a belt, or risk losing your pants.

On a day trip we took the train from Lausanne to Como, in northern Italy. It's only two hours away by train, but to get there you have to cross the Alps from north to south. You do that by taking the Simplon tunnel, which was dug in the nineteenth century and is still considered one of the greatest engineering feats of all time.

You leave Lausanne at 6 AM. It's rainy and cold and miserable. And two hours later you emerge in Como, and it's sunny and balmy and hot and there are real palm trees growing outside the train station.

And small coins are suddenly worthless in Italy because the country is undergoing a monetary crisis as a direct result of the abandonment of the gold standard. The government is incapable of producing valid paper money, so they authorize private banks to print their own. They are postage stamp-sized bits of shit printed on common bond paper on one side only, so if you drop one in a puddle it is ruined. The lowest denomination is 500 lire, which was worth about a dime, and when you went to the shops to buy cigarettes or a newspaper they would give you your change in candy or little boxes of wooden matches.

So Italian coins of 100 lire or less were lying about like gravel, and I picked up a few of those.

A few days later we travelled on to Rheinhousen in southern Germany to stay a while with family there, and after that we were on to London, England.

Back in Canada, I had read a book that was written for budding young coin collectors like me. It was published in Britain, and it suggested that the best way for a young boy to start up a coin collection was to simply rummage through a farmer's field after it was ploughed. That struck me as absolutely the stupidest thing that I had ever heard of, until I got to England, where people actually earn a decent living doing exactly that.

Every square inch of the entire country is a lasagna of archeology from the Stone Age up to now, and metal objects from the Bronze Age up to the present routinely appear after a decent ploughing, including hordes of roman coins, piles of Saxon jewellery, swords and spears from the Norman conquest, and so on up to the present.

But I didn't have the time or the equipment or the knowhow to rummage about in a farmer's ditch, so I just rummaged through my own pocket change.

As it happened I arrived at a crucial moment. For centuries the Brits had used a monetary system based on no less than the ancient Babylonian base-sixty number system. To both of their credits, it allowed them to compute extremely large numbers without the aid of electronic devices, and it enabled them to devise a very precise calendar and clock that we still use today.

But the brits decided once and for all to switch their old money to a decimal system. Their conversion deadline was February 1971, and I landed right smack in the middle, when the old money was being phased out and the new money was being phased in, and both systems were in use simultaneously. It was absolute fucking chaos.

My collection of small change from that time would fit into your fist, but the stories that they tell could fill libraries.

Let's start with the old money. The basic unit was one penny, and it was a massive coin by any standard. 1¼ inch in diameter, it is bigger than most coins in circulation today, and whereas the exact same design was standard throughout the colonies including Canada and Australia, everyone abandoned it a hundred years ago in favour of a smaller coin, but it remained legal currency in the British Isles well into the twentieth century.

Below The penny is the half-penny, another massive copper coin, and below that is the farthing, or quarter-penny, which is about the size of our own now-defunct Canadian penny, and features a very angry-looking English robin on the obverse. Below that still is the half-farthing, or one-eighth of a penny.

This one is a total conundrum. I found one in almost perfect condition in my pocket change, even though it is dated 1844 and features a perfect profile of a very young Queen Victoria with her very short hair tied up in a tight tiny bun behind her head with ribbons, the way you would coif a child. And they were officially retired from circulation in 1870, exactly one hundred years before it casually appeared in my pocket, in near-mint condition.

And what, precisely, can you actually buy with one-eighth of a penny?

Above the penny were higher denominations. The next up was a three-penny coin, officially three pence (pence being the plural of "penny"), which was known as a three-penny bit or thrupny, and pronounced exactly as I wrote it. It's an ugly little twelve-sided coin, thick and obnoxious, with far less copper in the brass alloy so that it looks yellow, but not gold-yellow. Just green-yellow, like bat puke.

Above the thrupny is sixpence. That's worth six pence.

Two sixpence make 12 pence, and pence are abbreviated lower-case d, which is an upside-down lower-case p, so the guy at the mint was either dyslexic or drunk or both.

12 pence is written 12d, but 12d adds up to a shilling, which is the next coin on the list. A shilling is 12 pence, or 12d, and it is abbreviated lower-case s. The Cockneys call it a Bob.

If you see a sign that reads 2s 4d, that's two shillings fourpence, or twenty-eight pence. If it reads 2s 4d ½, that's two shillings four and a half pee, and if it reads 2s 4d ¾ that's two shillings four and a half pee faaathing because you have to add on the ¼ cent (farthing) to the half-pee to get to ¾ pee but you have to add the farthing the way that Greta Garbo would pronounce "Daaahling."

What comes after a shilling? Well, two shillings, actually. But they don't call it that. They call it a Florin. They also have a double Florin, which is, you guessed it, four shillings. Next comes a half-crown. That's worth five shillings, or two florins and one shilling, or one double florin plus a shilling, or something like that. After the half-crown comes the full crown, and there are five in one pound which is worth 240d (pronounced pee). One crown is worth exactly 48p.

Then you have a sovereign, which is worth twenty shillings or one pound or 240 pee, and after that you've got a guinea which is worth 21 shillings or 252 pee.

That's the old money, and thank god they simplified it. Back in the day they had ¼ farthings so you would need about four thousand of those before you had a pound, and it would actually weigh about twenty pounds. But they also had 1/3 farthings and three ha'pneys, that is to say, a coin that was worth exactly and precisely one and a half pence.

I didn't have to rummage around in a farmer's field to find a panoply of exotic coins; I just had to empty my own pocket.

Simultaneously with the old money was the new decimal money, or new pence, or NP, which they had decided to introduce at the same time that they were withdrawing the old money, so both were simultaneous legal tender.

Now a pound was worth 100NP instead of 240p. They ditched the faaahthing and kept the ha'pny but made it exactly the same size as the former half-farthing, tossed out the thrupny but introduced the tuppence (2NP) which was exactly identical in size to the old ha'pny but was worth 4.8p, and the sixpence, now worth 2.5 NP, had to go. And now 5NP was worth a shilling, or Bob, 10NP was worth a florin, 20NP was worth two florins or one crown, 50NP was worth 12 shillings, or Bobs, each worth either 12p or 5NP, or two crowns and a florin. Or maybe one half-crown, a shilling, a 10NP, a sixpence, a 3p or thrupnee, a 5NP, a couple of 2NP and a few faaathings. Now how much change does the vendor owe you on a purchase labelled 2s 4 3/4d - 25.5NP if you pay either with a 50NP coin or with an old crown? And which of the two prices is the cheapest?

Welcome to London in 1971.

But my favourite by far was the four-penny coin. It was popular in the Middle Ages and was briefly revived in the Edwardian age, but since they couldn't realistically call it a frupny, they simply baptised it the groat. They had been removed from circulation centuries ago, except for the maundy groats, so I didn't actually have any in my pocket change, but I mention it for its curious cultural history.

Maundy groats were typically minted at Easter or Christmas, and in a precocious form of social welfare were handed out to the poorest among the population (the mendicants, or "maundies" to spend as they pleased. British royalty still distribute ''maundy money", a symbolic gesture of gratitude, particularly to war veterans.

So what exactly is a groat, anyways? It is basically de-husked grain. If you translate groat to French, you get "gruau," which literally means, oatmeal. That's the top scratch. Let's dig a bit more.

In Victorian England, a groat was synonymous with a pittance or a number too small to be considered serious or valuable. "I don't give a groat" was a popular reply when you really didn't give a sweet flying shit. The word continued to evolve, and by the 1960's it came to be synonymous with "finger pie," that is, digital penetration of a vagina as a poor alternative to actual sex, but better than nothing at all. "I got a groat" literally meant, I inserted my fingers, but not my penis.

In the classic 1967 Beatles song "Penny Lane," John Lennon sings "Four of fish and finger pie." The "four of fish" is 4 pence worth of fish and chips, which is the poor man's portion, the smallest portion that you can buy, and the "finger pie" is as far as you can get with a girl who doesn't want to go all the way, but when you withdraw your fingers they smell like fish. They are actually called "fish fingers," or, a "Groat." So 4d. or four pence (a groat) (fruppence) is associated with some kind of failure, or making do with a small victory when a higher aspiration has been thwarted.

I've enjoyed a few groats in my life and I hope to enjoy a few more before I die. Maybe 'fruppence" will someday become a real word, but meanwhile, it's just worth a groat.

BLOOD MONEY AND DÉJÀ-VU

One day, back in 1971, while visiting family in Switzerland, we went on a day trip.

There was a paddle-wheel steam boat that sails around the Lac Leman, which is a very big lake that straddles the border between Switzerland on the north side and the Haute Savoie (French Alps) on the south. The boat trundles slowly around the lake, and you can get off whenever you like, visit the new town, and then get on again and trundle on to another destination. Lausanne is on the north shore, about midway in the middle, in Switzerland.

Evian, where the water comes from, is directly opposite, on the French side. When we got to Evian, we disembarked and I asked my aunt if we could go to the bank to buy some french coins for my collection. All I wanted was a few centimes, maybe one of each denomination from one centime up to a whole franc. (about 25 cents worth).

She indulged me, although she clearly thought that the request would be too trivial to bother a bank clerk with. At the counter a very polite old lady greeted us. My aunt bothered to mention that I was family from Canada, and that I collected coins. That prompted a response that I could not have ever provoked short of shoving a steam-powered dildo up her ass. She gladly converted my single swiss franc into french pennies, then asked me to wait a minute while she went back to her office.

Here you go. She held forth a tiny lidless wooden box that looked as if it had survived the Napoleonic wars, which it probably had. The bottom of the box was covered with a small pile of tiny metal discs, each one as pathetic as its neighbor. Small, unidentifiable black coins covered with mildew. Some of them were stuck together with rust. If I had been old enough to understand sex, I would have ejaculated on the counter. To me, every one of those bits of dross were solid gold.

How much, my aunt asked, expecting to pay.

Oh no. You can have them. They're worthless. Usually we just throw them in the garbage.

That was a barefaced lie, on both counts. Those coins had been sitting in the bottom of that box at the bottom of her desk drawer for decades, possibly generations. She hadn't just diligently stowed them away from childhood to near-retirement because they were worthless and destined to be discarded, although technically there was less than five cents' worth of metal in the entire stack. She had intentionally hidden that minute pile of slag in the hopes that some day someone would come to her and liberate her from her charge.

She dumped the tiny pile of filthy infected unidentifiable metal discs onto the counter, but kept the box. Presumably it was worth more than its contents, and my aunt felt a sudden impulse to wash her hands. She is Swiss, after all.

Back in Canada, I looked over my new-found hoard, sorted them as best I could. These particular coins seemed very strange to me. Where the inscriptions were legible through the decades-old patina, they described in foreign languages and strange alphabets place names that have long since been erased from the world atlas.

There are details about the contents of the battered wooden box from Evian that I never understood, until very recently. As I grew older my interest in this childish hobby dwindled, and I in turn relegated them to a small box in a dark corner of the attic, where they sat for another half-century.

Recently I repatriated them, and with a better understanding of world history and the advantage of Google, I began to unravel their secrets.

A coin from Austria from 1943 with a German swastika proudly displayed. One from the independent republic of Moldavia and Bohemia from the time of the Nazi regime in the Sudetenland. A few zinc coins from Nazi-occupied Netherlands. Several pieces from French colonial north Africa, the Maghreb (Algeria, Morocco and Tunisia). A proud portrait of Generalissimo Francisco Franco.

That fucking little nasty filthy war-torn wooden box contained a brief history of ruthless colonialism and brutal fascist domination, and the historical proof is shamelessly stamped onto every single tiny damaged metal disc in that grungy little container. No wonder the initial impulse was to throw them all away, to discard them forever, as though they were evil talismans, tangible proof of the devil's power over the minds of men. The justification would have been that the monetary value of the contents was close to zero, and that is still true today, fifty years later.

But coins are propaganda disguised as wealth, and always have been. Fealty to the image on the coin, whether a God or an emperor or a king, or an ideology represented by a simple symbol, was requisite to earning it.

Simply discarding those deceptively simple objects would not do. The incarnate evil would endure, and eventually manifest itself elsewhere, like the Ring of Mordor.

But some cooler heads prevailed, and the old lady in the bank at Evian was one of them. She and her family would have been witness to and victims of the atrocities committed in Europe over centuries. An innocent, angel-haired little kid from Canada showed up looking for coins, any coins, and she must have thought, now's my chance to safely pass on this demonic legacy.

This child is innocent of our parents' sins; perhaps his small hands and curious eyes and simple heart will be impervious to the dark message contained within. Perhaps he can purge the evil.

Kinda like Frodo Baggins.

That tow-haired little kid is past sixty years old now, more silver than gold on top, more Gandalf than Frodo, with the cane and the beard but minus the hat, although it would do nicely to cover the bald spot, and I am only just beginning to understand the legacy that that old woman left me. A handful of tiny, badly manhandled brass discs, survivors of war, each one firmly, permanently stamped with a message of hope or hatred, of love for the homeland or contempt for its occupants. Tiny little windows into our ugly and brutal past.

Some discover a hoard under a farmer's field. I stumbled upon a tiny slice of history that most would prefer to forget, but all are compelled to remember.

I have yet to cast them into the fires of Mordor, because I believe that they still have the ability to empower us. Just as the old woman in the bank both cherished and denigrated them, for an entire generation or longer, waiting for the day when the Messiah would spontaneously appear and rid her of her burden, both worthless, and yet priceless.

BUTTONS

I LIKE BUTTONS.

When I was a kid, every family had a button box.

All of our parents were post-WWII immigrants from poor families from pretty much every country in western Europe, so recycling absolutely everything was just what you did. Children wore hand-me-downs and rummage sale clothes until they literally disintegrated, and then the garments' components were disassembled.

The worn cloth was used as dishrags and mops and window cleaners, or cut into strips to tie up the tomato plants or even as impromptu field dressings when a child came home with a bloody knee or elbow after playing outdoors all day, falling out of a well-climbed tree in quest of ripe wild fruit, or crashing their bike face-first into the ditch without any protective gear whatsoever while dare-racing down a long, steep, gravel-clad hill.

And even when the rags had long outlived any possible human function, they were not discarded. The remaining rags ("*lambeaux*," or shreds, in popular parlance) were hand-cut into long thin strips, and then tightly tressed together into long cords. The cords were then painstakingly hand-stitched in a spiral pattern, and the result was a thick carpet or throw-rug commonly known as a "*Tapis tréssé*," or weaved carpet.

And the solid stuff, the buttons and clasps and zippers and buckles, were all painstakingly unstitched and stored away for future use. Into the button box.

In 1961 I was two years old and my parents seriously considered moving back to the Old Country. We took a steam ship. (Not a modern-day cruise ship, but an actual passenger vessel with huge smoke stacks like the Titanic.) Only rich people took the airplane; the rest of us took the boat.

Since our family sabbatical was to last an entire year, my dad decided that I needed a decent set of clothes. A single outfit, respectable enough to be worn in polite company, but durable enough to withstand the dirty, withering wear-and-tear of multi-seasonal outdoor hard play that two-year-old brats will inevitably indulge in.

Every single copper penny of the household budget had already been earmarked for the cost of the passage overseas, so buying new clothes was out of the question. He had to design and manufacture the costume himself, using only what he could find at hand.

He settled on an old winter coat that my mother had worn (in every dictionary sense of the word) ever since they stepped onto the boat that brought them to Canada a decade earlier. I suspect that it was already old at that time, probably acquired as a used hand-me-down during the war.

It was a garish thing, a tartan plaid that displayed every colour of the rainbow in various hues from bright yellow, fire-engine red and sky blue to brooding navy and burgundy and black, but the pure wool weave was virtually indestructible, aside from the decades of slow surface erosion on the collar and the elbows and the hem.

My dad patiently unstitched the garment back down to its original components. He now had the raw materials to recreate something else.

But the new garment had to be multifunctional. He knew that the nearly-indestructible cloth still had decades of life in it, but the resurrected costume had to fulfill a variety of criteria. It had to be formal enough for me to be presentable in polite company, but casual and versatile enough to allow me to play in pretty much any kind of weather, and sturdy enough to survive a child's natural activity for at least a year. And it all had to be designed and manufactured with everything that was sitting on the dining room table. And it all had to be accomplished before the boat left for Portsmouth.

If this sounds like a scenario for a reality TV show, it isn't. It's just plain, ordinary reality.

He decided on a three-piece suit. Pants, a vest and an overcoat. So he stood me naked on the kitchen table and diligently measured every part of my body, then transcribed the shapes and lines onto a large sheet of crepe paper with a boat-shaped hunk of chalk the size of my hand whose edge he routinely sharpened to a keen knife-point with a hand file on an old wooden plank that lay over the cast iron radiator in front of the window of the living room behind the black-and-white rabbit-eared TV that he used as an impromptu work bench, (the radiator, not the TV), squatting on a wooden stool that he had hand-hewn from other planks that he had found in the garbage.

That drove my mom crazy, because all of the dust and wood chips and filth and crap from his improvised workshop inevitably ended up on the living room floor.

The pattern was then laid over the cloth, and the various pieces were cut out with scissors and stitched together on a Singer sewing machine that was powered by a foot pedal. The final touches, the zipper for the pants, and the bright red plastic buttons, emerged from the sacrosanct button box like communion wafers, and patiently and carefully hand-stitched into the finished garment, as if my dad was a medieval monk painstakingly hand-copying a sacred text. We were now ready to travel!

While we were over there, somebody, I don't remember who, offered me a toy. It was a sort of imitation teddy bear, about a foot high, with a moulded rigid smiling plastic face that looked a lot like Mickey mouse. The soft body was stuffed with foam rubber and covered with a thin, smooth synthetic fabric in blocks of black, red and yellow. I loved that toy more than anything else in the entire universe.

When we came home a year later, we sailed on the maiden voyage of the Carmania, another steamship. I was three years old by then, and I actually have old photographs of my dad holding me upright on the top of the guard rails of the ship as we both gaze out at the icebergs that float around us in the frigid north Atlantic. In those old pictures, I am still wearing that outrageous rainbow-clad plaid overcoat, although you can't see the colours, because the pictures are all in black and white.

I was only three years old, but I remember the homecoming as if it was yesterday.

As the Carmania sailed up the Saint Lawrence river towards Quebec city, I could see the bridge that spanned the river to Lévis on the south shore, and it seemed so astonishingly small on the distant horizon, barely bigger than my own tiny thumb, in comparison to the monumentally high ship's smoke stacks that dominated the sky just behind me, and I thought to myself, there's not a chance in hell that this huge steam liner is gonna fit under that tiny little toy bridge.

When we finally approached Quebec City, all hell broke loose. Since this was the maiden voyage of the Carmania, a multitude of smaller craft filled the harbour to greet us and surrounded the big ship, blaring their horns, and crowds of people had flocked to the docks to wave their arms and flags and improvised banners and cheer like banshees. Circus cannons bombarded us with confetti and colourful paper spirals. The tugs and the fire boats all came out, their crews dressed in full regalia, brass buttons and epaulets polished to reflect the sun, and as their sirens wailed they sprayed us all on board with high-pressure hoses like a riot squad in crowd-control mode.

You might only be three years old, but an event like that will stick to your brain forever.

Before we had left home a year earlier, my mom had redistributed stuff that we couldn't take with us back into the diaspora community where we lived. When we finally got back to Montreal a year later, many of the things that she had voluntarily but reluctantly abandoned were repatriated.

Among them was the precious button box. It had been dutifully stored away by faithful friends and ceremoniously handed back upon our arrival, as if it had actually contained the last remains of a venerated ancestor.

And my beautiful multi-functional suit had fulfilled its tasks remarkably, but was now worn to the marrow and needed to evolve towards another, less noble vocation, like scrubbing the toilet. My dad couldn't bear to see it entirely debased to that humble condition, so before tearing it up and discarding it entirely, he started all over again.

He patiently unstitched the inglorious but almost indestructible wool fabric, just as he had done a year earlier with my mother's coat, then patiently removed the accessories and stoically discarded the hopelessly unusable parts, He then repeated the same process that I had undergone a year earlier, but this time the subject wasn't me, but rather my favourite toy.

He stood the foot-high doll up on the kitchen table and repeated the same ceremony, this time in double miniature.

The subject was duly measured, the shapes and sizes were transferred to the remaining shreds of woolen cloth with the fist-sized, razor-edged hand-honed chunk of chalk, the various pieces were hand-cut with giant scissors and dutifully stitched back together to form a perfectly tailor-maid little plaid suit for my favourite toy, complete with hand-stitched button holes to accommodate the bright red plastic buttons that had adorned the original. It was a miniature clone of the hand-made garment that I had worn daily for an entire year.

I still own that toy. If you saw it, without knowing its history, you would immediately toss it in the trash. One of my dogs mistook it for a chew toy and demolished the back of its head and ripped off the Mickey Mouse ears, but the rest of it survived, including the tailor-made suit.

I also still own the original button box, and its original contents. It's a small thing, about half the size of a shoe box, hand-weaved from mahogany-coloured rattan, or possibly bamboo, and it squeaks like a mouse when you open it. Inside is a random polyglot cacophony of buttons of every size, shape and colour, as well as a small pasteboard that harbours a needle and thread, and a tiny, delicate device designed to help you thread the needle.

I like to open it once in a while, sort and count the buttons, spread them all over the dinner table and feel them and smell them. I like to wonder about their past vocations, the shiny brass ones with embossed anchors and the tiny humble ones cut from a cow's horn, the wonderful clothes that they once so proudly adorned, and who wore them, and when, and why.

Then I toss them all randomly back into the box and put it all away, and go back to my real life.

If I die and you come across that box, do not casually discard it.

I sincerely believe that it harbours the spirits of my ancestors.

BRASS KNOBS

Hi.

My name is Carol.

When I was a child, I wanted to be a belly dancer, or a mermaid, or a princess, or both. But since my parents were chronic alcoholics and mostly divorced, I ended up as a waitress at the local snack bar. Then I figured out that old rich men would give me stacks of money for train fare to ride on the Bajungy Tunnel Express. And even though it's a dark, damp, one-way ticket, they just kept on coming.

Sometimes I pretended to like the men. We called it GFE, but it was only an extended warranty on my bartered consent, and it just cost them extra for exactly the same fucking thing.

Up until last week I was driving a Porsche and living in an upscale condo, all paid for in cash, until the SWAT team crashed down my door and bounced me down the stairs on my head by my hair and shoved me into a police cruiser and made me sleep on a hard, wooden bench for two days before I could see the judge.

But that's OK, cuz the judge had already paid for my Porsche, and my condo. Mostly all of the cops complimented me on my amazing breasts. The ones that were too shy to vocalize merely ogled them silently for free.

Nice boobs? Fuck'n' A; the judge had paid for most of

them, so they ain't no bargain basement Dollar-Store snap-ons. Solid brass, nickel-plated, turbo-charged twin carbs, chrome-wheeled, fuel-injected and steppin' out over the line.* With 24-carat solid gold sealed-bearing cherry-bomb self-lubricating frictionless friction nipples. Triple-grounded to avoid injury from static shock, and fully insured for civil liability in case of sudden death from cardiovascular or cerebral accidents during use. Guaranteed 5 years or 50 thousand kliks, whichever comes first.

You fuck with these puppies, you'll be dead before you hit the ground.

And when I die, I would like to be buried with them.

Thank you.

Carol.

Sorry Carol, but since we are divorced, I want the tits back. They cost me ten grand, and the (other) judge decided you have to reimburse all of my expenses before the kids were born, and since you can't actually cough up the cash, I want my boobs back. Both of them. By tomorrow.

Thank you.

Bob.

What the fuck you want with my boobs? You gonna wear them?

Carol.

I'll do whatever the fuck I want with them, since they legally belong to me. I'm thinking of mounting your rack on the wall over the fireplace with the other hunting trophies.

Bob.

---

*Bruce Springsteen "Born to Run," 1975.

Well, the OTHER judge paid for at least half of them, so you might be entitled to just one. Or maybe just part of one. You'll have to slice up the pie.

Carol.

See now, if Bob and Carol had had a pre-nup and a legal will, none of this would have ever happened. The value-added mammary improvements would have been included as part of the family patrimony, and eventually the children would have legally inherited the precious knobs, to dispose of according to their will.

So now we don't know if Carol will be buried with them, or just one of them, or part of just one of them, or Bob will hang them on his trophy wall, or the high-priced lawyers and accountants will have suckled all of the equity out of the Twin Towers, or the kids will simply pawn them off in order to buy crack cocaine.

And by then the paparazzi hovered all over the precious hooters like frequent flies on carrion luggage. They had made front page news worldwide, and the artisans who had hand-crafted them were suddenly claiming royalties.

Darned things, those breasts. I wonder who really owns them? We may never know.

What I do know is they were among the most elegant works of art that I had ever seen, comparable to a Fabergé ostrich egg.

No wonder everybody fought tooth and nail head to toe hand over fist nose to the grindstone to get their fingers on them.

BUCKETS

I LIKE BUCKETS.

Hank Williams famously sang, "My bucket's got a hole in it, I can't buy no beer."

For decades I assumed that the protagonist had some kind of job that required a bucket, and since said bucket was leaking, he was unable to work and therefore had no money to buy beer.

I learned differently when I visited Cuba during the Gulf War.

The wife and I were bored with the gated tourist resort, so we jumped the fence, illegally bought Cuban pesos from criminals on a shady street corner in Matanzas, and went underground, living with Cubans in their homes.

We ended up in San Antonio de las Banos, a suburb of Havana reserved exclusively for Cubans. We got there by riding the Wawa, the local bus, but it was so crowded that we had to hang from the window on the outside with our toes wedged onto the top of the rear wheel bumper, inches above the bouncing, churning tire. The local Cubans inside the bus held us up by our forearms through the open window lest we fall and perish under the wheels, limiting our potential injuries to a mere broken leg, rather than a slow and agonizing death.

When we arrived at our destination, our hosts, a young couple, both engineers, asked us if we would like to have a beer. After our ordeal we gladly consented, but since they didn't actually have any, they invited us to accompany them outside.

I naturally assumed that we were either going to a tavern or a bar, or maybe to a convenience store. The town, as we later learned, possessed neither. Instead, we walked towards the town square, and as we went, we met more and more residents who were all wandering in the same direction. When we arrived, half the town was standing about, greeting one another and indulging in idle chitchat and local rumours.

It was then that I noticed that everyone was holding some kind of container. Until then, I just assumed that they were bringing them to some kind of recycling facility. But no.

After a few moments, a cistern truck drove into the town square in a cloud of dust and the driver killed the engine. The driver disembarked, walked to the back of the truck, and deployed a pistol similar to the one you use to fill up your gas tank.

The people dutifully lined up behind the truck and the driver then began to pump beer from the truck into everyone's container. Some of them were buckets. People gratefully folded a few bronze coins into the driver's hand, even though the service was free.

Then everyone moved on to a beautifully arranged public space next to the river, complete with gazebos and park benches and picnic tables. The blood-warm, unpasteurized beer was slowly and respectfully shared along with neighborly conversation. When the buckets were empty, everyone returned home to prepare the evening meal.

A few years ago, I had a conversation with someone who is very dear to me. The person had a good career and a nice house in a nice neighborhood and grown-up children that were prospering. But there was some malingering issue, some kind of feeling of unfulfillment, as if the sacrifices made to achieve the middle-class dream had left a hole in their soul.

'It's the bucket list," they said.

The wha!?

You know, the bucket list. The list of stuff that you want to do before you die, before you kick the bucket.

I had never heard of the bucket list, and hearing about it for the first time, it struck me as absolutely the stupidest thing that I had ever heard of in my entire life. You get born, you get to do shit while you're alive, you make choices, some of them are good and others are absolutely terrible, and then you get dead. Same as absolutely everybody else. That's democracy.

Pride and shame in being me, from womb to tomb, with all of my petty victories and spectacular failures; that was all I could aspire to. How is a wish list going to change any of that, unless your wish is to cure disease, stop wars, and bring peace and harmony and health and prosperity to the planet? Lofty objectives, well beyond the reach of pretty much everybody. Exactly how hang gliding over Machu Picchu during a solar eclipse will change any of that is beyond me. It just struck me as so hopelessly selfish, narcissistic and self-indulgent.

But I shut my mouth and listened. That's the best way to learn.

As the conversation went on, I realized that this person did not want to create something unique; They didn't want to write a poem or plant a cherry tree. They merely wanted to consume or use up or gain ownership of something that they perceived to be unique, even though it wasn't.

Most of the items on the wish list were merely exotic destinations that had to be acquired at great financial expense. They had to be purchased and collected, like exotic jewels, or stamps in a stamp collection, or indulgences paid in cash to the Holy Church in exchange for pardons for unpardonable sins and a first-class ticket to paradise without the inconvenience of contrition.

There was something grotesque and obscene about the innocent mask that pretended a desire for purity and knowledge but which hid a voracious ogre that only wanted to devour the entire banquet, then thump its chest and proclaim victory.

I would have liked to say that the greatest treasures are the ones that you share unselfishly with others, not the ones that you hoard for yourself. And the greatest acts of charity are those that go unseen.

But I was there to listen, not to speak.

BOB THE DUCK

Bob is a rescue duck. And not even a real wild duck, but one of those plump white hybrid Peking ducks that are designed and raised in captivity by men in order to end up on your dinner plate within four months of hatching.

What was Bob doing on a frozen, snow-covered pond in mid-November a couple of miles from my house? Waiting for imminent death, obviously.

It started on a Saturday afternoon.

A woman, middle-aged and teary-eyed, knocked on my door.

"Are you the chicken lady?" she whimpered.

"Um, no. That would be my wife. Let me get her."

Louise got the moniker because we were the first in our community to adopt chickens. It was controversial; some neighbours frowned while others delighted. The reason for that is because we let the chickens roam free, so they were constantly crossing the road to get to the other side, and some commuters were charmed and others were annoyed, and ditto for the neighbours who ended up with chickens roto-rooting their flower beds in search of tasty worms.

There was even a law case when a neighbour took us to court because a few of our intrepid birds were found on his property. He called the police and they had to give us a ticket, and a warning. Make sure the next time we come back it's for something worthy of the badge and the gun.

We contested the ticket and won our case, essentially guaranteeing us the right to keep our animals for eternity.

The lady from up the hill knew us by reputation, and after a cup of hot tea and a box of tissues she emptied her bag.

Up the hill from us there is a natural pond that is teeming with wildlife, including wild ducks. There is a wooden footbridge that spans the pond, and our guest lives on the other side.

All summer long parents and children delighted in feeding the ducks with bread, tossing crumbs from the bridge and watching as the ducks paddled about to retrieve them.

But in winter the pond is about as popular as an underground parking garage. The native fowl have all taken wing for southern climes, the water is ice-bound, and the children have homework to do and video games to play.

But Bob can't fly. He got left behind, by the wild ducks, and by the children. Starvation, exposure, and hungry predators were Bob's fate, and the clock was ticking. It was a matter of days. Perhaps hours. We may already have been too late.

We were more than willing to adopt the forlorn duck, but first we had to catch the bugger. Since it was Saturday afternoon and the pale winter sun was waning, we agreed to attempt an intervention the following morning.

The next morning was sunny and bitching cold. We drove up the hill armed with only a bag of white sliced bread and a bath towel. We could have walked up in a few minutes, but if our quest was successful, I lurched at the idea of carrying a twenty-pound angry feral duck back down the hill in my arms.

We met our newly met neighbour at the top of the hill, then negotiated some backyard trails to the pond and the bridge, where the lady's husband joined us.

From the top of the bridge we gazed out at the wunnerful wiener wunnerland. Frozen white ice covered with thick white snow for as far as we could see. White on white on more fucking white for eternity, Amen. Finding a single white duck in that blinding wilderness seemed impossible.

Then my wife Louise had an idea. She grew up on a farm with all kinds of critters big and small, cows and chickens and hogs and dogs, most of which were allowed to wander about the vast property at will. One of her jobs as a child was to call them all back home at the end of the day, and she knew a simple chant that usually worked charms.

She cupped her mouth with her hands and began to hog-holler, "*Viens-t'en viens! Viens-t'en viens t'en viens!*" In English, that's like Bob Barker on *The Price is Right* barking: "Come on down!"

And sure enough, after a few minutes, there was a tiny white blob on the blinding white horizon that seemed to be waddling slowly towards us. It was Bob.

When Bob got to the bridge, we tossed down torn-up chunks of white sliced bread and talked up a storm so that he could hear us and know that there were people around, assuming that that would reassure him.

Half the job was done. We had found Bob. Or rather, Bob had found us.

But his new home was a mile away, and he wasn't about to go without a fight. The other half of the battle, the big half, was yet to be.

Since Bob was not about to miraculously fly up onto the bridge, I and the other man had to crawl down the treacherous, snow-bound slope to the river bank to get closer to our subject.

The pond was frozen over in the middle, but the ice was too thin to support our weight, and there was a three-foot gap of open, frigid, fast-moving water between us on the steep slippery bank and the ice-bound duck. My outstretched arm and the duck's slender neck formed a perfect bridge over the abyss, with the tender bit of soft white bread at the apex, but we were no nearer to reaching our goal.

We changed our tactics. We sat on the frozen bank and allowed our feet into the icy stream, then I held aloft the tender treats to the left while my companion reached discreetly from the right and, when Bob stretched out his long slender neck to reach the food, the other man struck out like a cobra and grabbed poor old bob by the throat and pulled like hell. The next few seconds were total chaos. Bob honking, wings flapping, men pulling, feet sloshing, ice water splashing, thin ice cracking, frozen butts sliding, and total disaster was averted when I managed to wrap the whole cold white feathered barking mess into the beach towel.

I carried the thoroughly mummified Bob back to the car and drove him to his new home. But before we could integrate him into the chicken coop, Louise thought that it would be a good idea to give him a bath.

Why I actually agreed with her still amazes me. Usually I'm smarter than that. But I love my wife, for better or worse till death do us fart, so I routinely will acquiesce to her outrageous and unreasonable claims and pretend that it's a good idea. You all should try that sometimes; it often leads to unprecedented and totally unpredictable adventures and cleverly sidesteps potential divorce opportunities.

We filled up the bathtub with lukewarm water and dumped The Bob inside.

Hoo boy. That duck has a wingspan wider than my outstretched arms, and pec muscles that pound-for-pound would make Stallone or Schwarzenegger look like girl scouts. We took a shower, and so did the entire bathroom.

Then we let the duck wander around the house and explore. He spent some time arguing with himself in front of the full-length mirror in the bedroom before joining my dog on the couch in the living room watching *The Simpsons* on TV. I think he really appreciated the *Itchy and Scratchy* bit.

The next day we introduced him to the chickens by dumping him into the chicken coop. Usually chickens push back at interlopers; they have their own strict hierarchies, but Bob was big and loud and surprisingly conciliatory. By spring he was king of the harem, telling the chickens what to do and how and when and where to do it, and the chickens seemed to spontaneously accept him as their new leader.

Now allow me to skip ahead a few months.

The following autumn, the migratory birds were again heading south, and as they deployed in their formations and quacked out their orders, Bob became agitated. He would run about the property and whack loudly at the volatile passers-by, either admonishing them for abandoning him or pleading with them for a chance to join the train. He would even leap up on to large stones that lay about the property, presuming that the extra elevation would allow his voice to be better heard by the lofty transients.

But it was all in vain. Poor old Bob returned to his coop and consoled himself in the knowledge that the chickens down here on the ground actually depended on him.

Life is often full of little ironies, in case you haven't already noticed.

Following our lead, many neighbours adopted chickens. Some spent fortunes on custom-made chicken coops. Absolutely all of them forgot that, when winter comes, it gets cold and there's snow and you want to go on holiday.

They would routinely ask us to keep their chickens for the winter. They clearly had no idea about how chickens organize themselves. These beasts are not household decorations; they are living breathing thinking animals, and they have very strict rules about hierarchy. One of them is, last one in gets shit on. The newcomers eat last and get the worst roosting spots. And yes, they literally get shit on.

The highest roosts are reserved for the poultry aristocracy, and the lower echelons just beneath are occupied by the avian hoi-polloi, and the laws of gravity dictate a unidirectional outcome.

The chickens can move up in the hierarchy by fighting for a place, but often they just assume the roles that they are given by the higher-ups.

One day in October a neighbour asked us to take in his three chickens for the winter and we complied. Naturally his three chickens were low on the totem pole vis-à-vis our own brood, and the first two weeks were rough on them. Often, they were reluctant to return to the roost, knowing that they would be treated poorly.

One cold evening in early November Louise and I were curled up in front of the TV with a hot dinner and our trusty dog by our side when the dog began to bark.

I got up and the dog led me to the door. I put on my boots and coat and went outside, and there was Bob the Duck, whacking and quacking like the universe was on fire.

Usually the chickens all come home to roost at sunset, and Bob is the last one in, and then we close the door. Once Bob is in, the day is over.

But Bob refused to enter the coop and continued to make a fuss. I went back into the house to get a flashlight and then counted the chickens in the coop.

We were one chicken short, and daylight had abruptly ended.

Chickens fuel on daylight. In the morning, when the sun comes up, a little switch in their brains gets turned on and they instantly become hyperactive, and then remain like that all day until the sun goes down. Then they switch off and turn into zombies.

One of our chickens had been reluctant to return to the coop at sunset, and had probably been taken short somewhere in the underbrush and had promptly and abruptly fallen asleep. But where?

I and the dog went down the path into the woods with only the flashlight to guide us, but my puppy sniffed out the vagrant volatile in record time and we carried the poor animal back to the coop and parked her on a perch and then Bob, satisfied that his entire herd was accounted for, shut the fuck up and waddled back into the coop and chose his own spot to sleep, not too far up but safely away from under the roosting chickens, and I closed the door for the night.

Bob was missing a chicken, and he told the dog. The dog then told me that the duck was upset. Then I and the dog went out and found the missing chicken, without which the goddam duck would still be out there honking away as if he were witness to the Second Coming. (That's Jesus H. Fucking Christ in the flesh, for those of you who never benefitted from the proper proprieties of Saturday morning Baptist Bible school in lieu of heathen pagan soul-corrupting Loony Tunes cartoons.)

That's the day that I learned that ducks know how to count, and that animals of different species all talk to each other exactly the same way that people do.

Maybe even better, sometimes.

ACKNOWLEDGEMENTS

I acknowledge the universe for allowing me to exist and be able to spell the word ACKNOWLEDGEMENTS.

Don't try that at home, kids. You will injure yourself!

ABOUT THE AUTHOR

David Sapin lives in Saint Jerome, Quebec, where he raises free-range chickens and monarch butterflies and rescues feral cats. He doesn't mow his lawn or rake his leaves because he wants the wild bugs and critters to prosper. He deliberately feeds the raccoons and the skunks and the squirrels and the birds, because we are the interlopers, not them. He also hands out twenty-dollar bills to homeless people rather than contributing to bullshit tax-deductible charities that waste our money on bullshit that just pays for expensive bureaucrats and their fat pensions but fails to house or feed the homeless.

Printed by Imprimerie Gauvin
Gatineau, Québec